Write Naked

PETER GOULD

Write
Naked

MELANIE KROUPA BOOKS
FARRAR, STRAUS AND GIROUX / NEW YORK

Copyright © 2008 by Peter Gould
All rights reserved
Distributed in Canada by Douglas & McIntyre Ltd.
Printed in the United States of America
Designed by Jay Colvin
First edition, 2008
1   3   5   7   9   10   8   6   4   2

www.fsgkidsbooks.com

Library of Congress Cataloging-in-Publication Data
Gould, Peter L.
    Write naked / Peter Gould.— 1st ed.
        p.   cm.
    Summary: When Victor finds an old Royal typewriter at a yard sale
and takes it to his uncle's isolated cabin in the Vermont woods to
attempt to write, he meets up with an unusual girl, and together they
explore their concerns about the world, themselves, and each other.
    ISBN-13: 978-0-374-38483-8
    ISBN-10: 0-374-38483-5
    [1. Writing—Fiction.   2. Typewriters—Fiction.   3. Identity—
Fiction.   4. Interpersonal relations—Fiction.   5. Global warming—
Fiction.   6. Vermont—Fiction.]   I. Title.

PZ7.G7356Wr 2008
[Fic]—dc22
                                                          2007016023

*This book is dedicated to
the residents of Woodchester, Vermont
(population 3)*

Write Naked

i'm where i never expected to be.

i'm in this cabin in the woods in the middle of the night. Half a mile at least from the nearest house. i've been here lots of times before, but never like this.

i'm not alone.

i look over at her, and it's almost too much, what i'm seeing. It is too much, so i look away, look back down.

She and i have never been here after dark before. That's what makes it especially magical. The only light is from an old kerosene lantern, like the kind they used to wave out on the platforms when a night train pulled in. It's up on a beam, hanging from an old nail. You have to take it down and trim the wick all the time so it doesn't smoke a lot. We had some candles, too, but they burned out.

There's also moonlight. The moon is full, which is why we came up here. The windows are open. Outside, through the screens, i can hear an owl, a breeze shaking the leaves, and the waterfall that's so small you could walk right by it and not see it, but you can hear it. It's just a few steps away from the porch.

There's one sound inside: this ROYAL typewriter.

Yes, t y p e w r i t e r.

It's really old, but it works. It prints letter by letter on typing paper. It's like a little word factory that's actually still in business, not boarded up like the old factories down in town. And it's noisy like factories used to be, with thumping metal, and springs pulling back and then letting go, and the chime that goes off at the end of every line, like there's this miniature worker inside whose only job is to whack the little bell every time you've gone seventy-four spaces, even if you're right in the middle of a word.

How i found this machine, and all that happened after that, is pretty much all i've been thinking about for the last two months. Sometimes i get so lost in it now--that story, i mean--that i almost forget i'm not alone.

That's hard to do tonight.

i used to be alone when i first came here, and sometimes, when i'm deep into my writing, it feels like i still am. Time goes by, and then i remember all of a sudden where i am, and who i'm with, and i come back up. Because besides the noise this old truth machine makes, and the sounds from outside, i suddenly notice the sound of her fountain pen, scratching across the paper. i never knew a pen could make that much noise.

i focus on that now, because it just stopped. So i look up again and stare across the table at her. She looks right back at me, kind of raising her eyebrows and tilting her chin to the side. i call it her slanted look.

i try to look just at her face.

"Are you having a hard time concentrating?"

She doesn't actually say this but i know that's what she's thinking. i can usually tell what she's thinking. Especially when she's smiling, like she is now.

Absolutely on purpose, making her point, she pushes her chair back and lets her arms hang down at her sides, not crossing them over her chest, not hiding, shoulders high and proud, inviting me, and i try hard, really hard, not to look at her BODY--whoops, accidentally hit the cap-shift key four times in a row. Note to myself: Don't look at her too hard. Focus on the writing. That's part of our deal.

i do sneak one quick look back, though, wanting to take it all in at a glance--her body in the lantern light--you want to hold on to the memory of the first time in your life you see that up close--but i want all the rest, too: the way everything in the cabin looks with the moon coming in. i swear. i really want to see it all. So i won't forget.

But i'm staring. i can't help it. She gives a big sigh. Then turns slowly away from me, to look out the window.

Her last page is on the table, waiting for me to read it.

She writes and draws with a fountain pen. It may be even older than my typewriter. When it runs out of ink, she sticks the point in a bottle of special ink and squeezes something and it makes a sound like our lips and tongues make when we kiss.

You can actually read her handwriting, it's that neat. i mean compared to mine when i write. She doesn't need lined paper. And you can tell where she stopped to think for a while--a long while--because some of the letters get curlicued ends going all over the page, and the o's get eyes and smiles, and a t will have a crossbar that twists upward and weaves through the line above it like some kind of vine, with leaves and all.

i type a last sentence. In a minute i'll pull the paper out of my machine, send it over to her to read. She's read all the other pages. Nobody else has read even one.

She'll read slowly, slower than she has to, for my benefit. It's to make me feel proud, like what i wrote must be important to her, as if she's pausing to consider every word. Like she'll know me better after each one. Like each word is a track some animal left on the ground, and she's following the trail back where it came from.

She does it to make us wait, too. i can feel that.

Wait for what?

When she's read it, she'll slide it back to me without saying anything, that's another part of our deal, and i'll put it away with all the rest in my backpack, she'll do the same with hers, and then i guess we'll both get up, and then--

And then i don't know.

It's up to her. She has the power.

We won't forget about the time. We promised.

Not that we have a watch or a clock. When the moon hits its highest point in the sky, that's the time.

To blow out the lantern.

Get dressed.

And head back down out of the woods.

1

April 17

i was riding my mountain bike up Greenleaf Street toward where it ends at the woods. In Vermont a spring Saturday morning means yard sales. i must have passed five of them. i kept right on going. i had no money in my pocket, and i was on my way to the bike trails.

There were cars parked on both sides of the street, and people getting out to check out the stuff: old cameras, beater bikes, half-wrecked chairs. i wove through them. But just where the street levels off a bit and you can take a breath, i stopped.

There was this little brick house on the left with a yard sale sign in front, and that's where i saw it, kind of tilted on the ground beside some army clothes, and a pile of sweaters someone had already mussed up. An old typewriter. It didn't holler at me, but it almost felt like it did, or maybe it typed "v i c t o r" with six quick noisy strokes on its own keyboard.

It was a big antique manual, all shiny black and made of heavy steel; you could tell that without picking it up. There was gold printing (R O Y A L) above the keys. Down on both sides there were two little plate-glass windows where you could look into the works.

i saw all this at a glance. i leaned my bike against a tree and squatted down and looked in one of the windows. There were all these levers, and hinges, and bars with little brass screws. It was a Writing Machine. No circuitry. No white plastic. Did they even have plastic back then? i bent down and heaved it up. It felt like it weighed more than my sister, Claire. She's ten.

This guy walked over to me. i had seen him once or twice before when I rode by, working around his house and yard. He had white hair and was wearing a checked flannel shirt. His eyes were kind of puddly and there were spots on his hands, but he had this nice smile, like your uncle holding two tickets to a Red Sox game behind his back.

"You like old typewriters?" he said, after i put it back down.

"Yeah, kind of. i mean, i like this one," i said. "They don't make them like this anymore." (Shoot, i thought, that really sounded stupid.)

"Do you want it?" he asked.

"No, i don't think so--" i started, meaning to explain that i didn't have any money.

He was way ahead of me. "You can have it, for free." Was it my imagination, or was he like some high priest up on a mountaintop with "I have been expecting you, My Son; here is Your Typewriter."

"i couldn't do that," i said. "It's for sale."

"Nobody wants it. Had it out last week, too. People don't use 'em anymore. My wife used to do typing at home, she learned on this one, then she got an electric. And then the computer. She's been dead five years."

"Oh," i said. i didn't know what else to say.

He went on. "I sold the electric a long time ago, but I kept this one around. Works perfect. Take a look; it's all cleaned up."

i put my face right down past the keys, there was this big opening like a half-pipe, where all the letters were lying side by side at the ends of their skinny metal arms and looking up at me upside down and backward. You could see it was all shiny where he'd scrubbed the letters--with a toothbrush, he told me--and there was an inky black ribbon, brand-new and hanging ready and straight where it went through a big silver clip. i pulled my head out and there were the keys, white enamel letters on round black buttons, each with a metal ring around it, and a long space bar with a low, worn spot where his dead wife's right thumb had hit it about five million times.

"Wow," i said. "It's beautiful."

i meant it.

He looked down, still smiling. He made a loose fist with his right hand and play-punched my shoulder. "Somebody else appreciates it. That's good. Go on; you take it home and go write a book. It's got a book in it."

"A book?"

"That's why I kept it around," he said. "Got a big story stuck in there, but I can't get it out. I'm too old."

"Okay," i said. "Thanks a lot." Now why did i say that? i was just passing by on my bike. i didn't need a typewriter. Another thing i didn't need was my mouth saying something before i've even thought about it. Usually i'm careful about what i say, and do. i like to think things out first.

The guy moved off to talk with another customer and left me sitting there beside that old writing machine. i was trying to catch up with what just happened. You know, you make what you think is a quick, harmless decision, and then the rest of your life gets immediately complicated in ways you can't even imagine. It was like some mysterious hand waved to me from a train, and i jumped on, without thinking, even though i didn't know where the train was going or who the hand belonged to.

And now i had a problem. Getting the typewriter home. Not only was it big and heavy but it was embarrassing, too. Who even bothers anymore with stuff that old and clunky? And i didn't want to call my mom or dad and say hey, could you come pick us up? Yeah, us. Me and my typewriter. i already wanted this old ROYAL to be hidden, as if keeping it secret was the first step to, i don't know, getting the story out. Yeah, i knew the guy meant it as a joke, but still--

i looked up at the blue sky. i needed to think.

i like logic problems, like the one with the guy and the river and the little rowboat and the dog and the chicken and the bucket of grain. You know, where you have to figure out how to ferry everyone across two at a time without them eating each other? i also like it when real problems--the kind you have to solve step by step--drop out of nowhere--well, somewhere--into my lap.

i'm sixteen. Just. i don't drive. In Vermont you can get your permit when you're fifteen, but i don't have mine yet. And even if i had it, you can't drive alone with a permit. My brother Will teases me about this, but i'm not in a hurry. i remember the scene in the kitchen after Will cracked up Mom's car, and i'm not anxious to replay that anytime soon. Anyway i like the anonymity of a bike. i'll do almost anything not to be noticed.

It's funny, cause i'm named for somebody who really wanted to be noticed. The Victor my folks had in mind when they named me was this singer-songwriter in South America who always fought for the poor and downtrodden. People who didn't have voices. His picture's hanging on our living room wall.

He was a national hero in Chile. He was so famous that when the army bombed their own White House, shot their president, and took over, Victor was the next person they went looking for. He could have run away and saved himself, but he stayed. They herded him and about two thousand other people into a soccer stadium, then brought him out in front of all those people and pounded his hands to a bloody pulp with their rifle butts. He was on his knees. They screamed, Sing, you son of a whore, so he did. But he didn't do it alone. As soon as he started, everyone in the whole stadium stood up and sang with him. They were all crying. Then the soldiers tortured him and dumped his dead body out on the street. His music has been playing in my house since before i was born.

i live with my mom and dad, and Claire. My brother Will goes to college. He picked a school really far away--i think on purpose--and we can't afford to have him come home often. He hasn't quite moved out of his room yet, but i'm next in line for it. i snoop around in there when i'm home alone. i guess i know just about every secret thing he's got hidden there.

Sometimes i sit in his big easy chair--another yard sale special--and read his college books. Textbooks in college cost a lot of money, way more than they're worth. It's some kind of scam, i think. So Will sells most of his to other students when he's done, but he holds on to all the books about how native people live or used to live. He's led me to <u>Ishi</u> and <u>Lame Deer</u> and <u>Black Elk Speaks</u> and <u>Tristes Tropiques</u>. That last one? It has a French title, but it's in English. It's worth it just to read the last chapter. i mean, if you want to read about inertia, entropy, and the end of the human mind, it's all there in one paragraph.

When i sit in Will's chair and read, it's like i've joined this special club. He said once, "Victor, if you read this stuff, you can save people in the past from drowning. It's like time is a river, and it's nighttime, and you can hear people calling, Help, we're disappearing! So you stop and listen. That's how you save them."

He tells me stuff like that, but he doesn't like to explain. i have to figure out what he means for myself. Maybe that's why i got off my bike. Maybe that old ROYAL did call me. Maybe you can save <u>things</u>, too.

2

So there i was, lying on the old man's lawn trying to figure out how to get the ROYAL home, watching cars and people coming and going. Carrying things. i was wondering if he was giving all his stuff away. All the people who got something smiling like now their lives were going to change.

i was thinking about Mr. Halliday's social studies class.

We studied the Vietnam War. We even took a bus trip down to D.C. to see the Vietnam Memorial. We got there early in the morning, stood parallel to the big open V, and Mr. Halliday talked about how it symbolized a wound we had, one that hadn't healed yet.

Some of the guys on the trip were snickering, even acting macho like if they'd been in the war they wouldn't have been so stupid, they wouldn't have died. But the memorial really got to me. It was black and shiny and heavy--just like the ROYAL.

Mr. Halliday told us about how he'd visited Vietnam and seen all different kinds of wounds--bomb craters, rips in the ground where someone heaved a bunker-buster down a tunnel. Villages where all you could see was a few stone walls, nothing else left.

Why was i thinking about all that?

You know how sometimes you have to circle back to figure out where a thought came from? i did that and arrived at the mountain bike. See, the U.S. Air Force pounded the country with B-52 bombers, and then by night the North Vietnamese resupplied. They moved all their war materiel south by bicycle, on what they called the "Ho Chi Minh Trail."

Ho was the leader of the Vietnamese, our enemy. He had a long skinny white beard, wrote poetry, and chain-smoked. He'd already beaten the Chinese and the French.

Ho's supporters would tie stuff onto their bicycles and start walking. Around the craters and land mines and through the defoliated jungle. In the dark. A whole parade of people wearing black, with mortar shells strapped to their bikes.

If the Vietcong could do it, i could, too. i picked up the word machine and heaved it onto the fork between the handlebars. Strapped it on with a couple of bungees. It wasn't going to be easy, but the ride was mostly downhill. i could balance it okay with my right hand on the ROYAL and my left on the nearest handlebar. So i started off, kind of wobbling. Figured i'd get used to it soon.

The yard sale guy peeled himself away from the people he was talking to and came over to stop me. He moved quicker than i thought he could.

"Hey, kid--" he said.

i stopped by the curb. "Yes?"

"I fought in Vietnam," he said. "Did you know that's how the Communists moved their supplies?"

"i know. That's where i got the idea."

He leaned his head real close to me. "I got this in the Central Highlands," he said, pointing to an old purple scar on his neck. "A half inch either way and I woulda bought it. Kicked a grenade away. Shoulda kicked it farther."

"Wow."

"We lost that war."

"i know." Some people don't think so, but i know we did. We're losing another one now.

He put one big hand on my shoulder. "We lost it because we had the B-52's and they had the bicycles. Don't you ever forget that."

"No, sir," i said. And then i thought to myself, Why did i say that? Sir, i mean. i never called anyone "sir."

"Vietnam's about the most friendly country in the world now," he said. "Almost ninety million people. Did you know that?"

"No, i didn't."

"Used to be a rat hole but not anymore."

i wasn't sure what he meant, but i nodded.

"What's your name?" he asked.

"Victor."

"Victor. Well, enjoy the writing machine. Go get that story out."

"Yeah, right."

"No, it's in there for sure. Hey, come back and show it to me when you got some of it written, okay?"

"Okay."

He reached out to shake my hand. i balanced everything for a second and stuck my hand out to his. A deal.

"Take it away," he said. "To the Victor go the spoils. You ever hear that?"

"Yes, sir." Just like i'd heard tons of stupid plays on my name. Like, Victor, the loser. Or, Hey, Victim, come over here.

"Good luck gettin' it home."

"Thanks."

It helped to pretend i was sneaking through the jungle. i moved down the hill from tree to tree. Just like the Vietcong. Even crossing Western Avenue, which usually has a lot of traffic, i don't think anyone noticed. i wheeled the bike and cargo into our garage. i undid the bungees, lifted the ROYAL off the bike, and pushed it onto a shelf. It joined a whole wall of stuff we have that's waiting for our yard sale.

It sat there looking sad, like it was the last one of its kind, and it was hoping i'd tell it that the rumor it had heard about the extinction of its species wasn't true. Sorry, i thought. The rest of your people are all dead. Then i covered it with a black plastic garbage bag.

You can see by now that i'm not totally normal. Like, i do what Miss Roth, my English teacher, calls "personification." Giving human voices and thoughts to things. i hear voices, too. Okay, not really voices. Call them messages.

We did the brain in biology class last fall, so i know that there's whole parts of our minds that we hardly ever use. i have a theory: i think these messages are signals from one of these unused parts. i hear them because i'm open to them. Sometimes they're like secret instructions, or random stuff i didn't know i knew.

Of course, listening for chance messages from my brain gets

me into trouble sometimes. People think i can't pay attention to what's right in front of my nose. They don't understand that if i'm not paying attention to what they want me to pay attention to, it's cause i'm paying attention to something else. And it could be really important.

Okay. i'd figured out how to get the ROYAL home. Now, logic problem number two. This teenager's got a mountain bike and a big old typewriter wrapped in a plastic garbage bag. He wants to keep it a secret from his mother, dad, and sister. He wants to get it out to his uncle's log cabin without anyone noticing. Yeah, that's what i decided i had to do.

That's what the message was saying.

3

April 23

Friday. i figured that would be the best day. To not be noticed, i mean.

Friday afternoons in spring, people stay around school for baseball, softball, track, ultimate Frisbee, or just lying around on the front lawn. Plus, there are these sidewalk bargain sales downtown. A lot of people go down there.

i went home--nobody there. i put on my old running shoes, loaded the ROYAL into my hockey bag and back onto the handlebars, and wheeled it up to the town bus route. Locked the bike to a tree and waited--nobody i know ever rides that bus. Well, they call it a bus, but it's maybe half the size of a real city bus. It's got bumblebees painted all over the side-- never could figure out why.

It came eventually, and i got on and scrunched down low in the seat, hoping nobody would see me ride by. A lady whose name i don't know, but i see her walk around town a lot with two shopping bags, she was the only other rider.

"That's a heavy load you've got there," she said.

"Yeah, it is," i answered, hoping that would be enough explanation.

It was. She got off before me. i rode another mile, out to the last stop by the fire station annex. That's where the bus turns around. Then i had to lug it on foot. After a while i couldn't believe how heavy it was.

i turned left on Bonnyvale Road, and then walked a few hundred yards up to old man Franklin's barn. The old man's in a nursing home, and he's not coming out. Not many people come through this neighborhood. It's mostly woods.

My plan was to stash the ROYAL in the barn, then ride out someday with my bike, and ferry it across Franklin's back field and up to my uncle's place, way up in the forest.

A long time ago, when my uncle Mo got back from Vietnam, he came to Vermont to visit my mother on the hippie commune where she lived. She told him there was this ten-acre "woodlot" for sale. In Vermont that's what we call a patch of forest that you can't get to and nobody wants. He wanted it, though. He hiked in, found a spring, and a zigzaggy stream coursing down from it, and almost every kind of tree he could think of.

He bought it and built a cabin on a ledgy spot right by the stream, so he could have fresh water.

If you don't know where this cabin is, it's almost impossible to find. That suited his purpose, and mine i guess--not that i had any idea what my purpose was. Well, i had some idea. It came with the typewriter. i didn't really understand it, but i knew there was one in there somewhere.

The cabin's up at the end of an old one-lane logging road

that comes off Franklin's pasture. There's no tire tracks anymore. Just a foot trail. By the time he'd cleared the road and
the house lot and trucked materials in and built the place,
Mom says Uncle Mo was pretty much cured of the war.

He moved out to Utah with a woman he met downtown.
They come back every once in a while, but the while keeps
getting longer. Now i guess i use the cabin more than anybody.

Mo's cabin would be a good place for me and my ROYAL,
but first i hid it in Franklin's old milking room under the barn.
i walked back to the main road, started toward town, and
then, instead of walking on the sidewalk, i climbed down a
stream bank and walked the rest of the way home splashing
my feet in the water and jumping from rock to rock.

Was i hiding, covering my tracks? Doing the Vietcong thing
again?

More like, i had always wanted to walk in the stream, and
here i was finally doing what i'd always wanted to do. Just because i had picked up that old typewriter. i liked that.

i also liked seeing the backs of the houses, and all the junk in
the yards. i liked the noise of the rushing water, too. And trying not to slip on the stones.

Most of all i liked the idea of choosing a different route
from the one i usually took. Like in that Robert Frost poem
Miss Roth, my English teacher, likes so much. i remember her
asking, "The road less traveled on. What is it a metaphor for?
What does it stand for, if it's not really a road?"

My Spanish teacher, Señor Iglesias, goes on about metaphors, too. He says there wouldn't be any language at all
without metaphors. Fifty thousand years ago, he says, some
woman was trying to explain something to a man. Men are

dense. So the woman had to invent a specific grunt that stood for the thing she was thinking about. And that's what still happens a thousand times a day in your brain.

"Every spoken thought," Señor Iglesias says, "is just a symbol for something inside your brain. This word, out here, is like that thought in there. But it's never exact. So, looking at it another way, every word you say is a lie."

That's probably why i think all the time and talk a lot less. i don't like to lie.

Now how did i get on that? Oh, right: walking home on the river, i had a feeling, and i was thinking of how to explain it to someone outside of me, if i ever needed to. i needed a metaphor.

i was way down low. No one walking or biking or driving on the road close by could see me. It was like i was flying under the radar.

Radar. Old World War Two spy technology. A little green TV screen glowing in the dark, and a minute hand sweeping around, picking out PT boats or fighter jets. Seeing you when you don't know you're being seen. i didn't want to show up on anybody's screen. i wanted to get low.

i sat down on a rock. The water rushed by me on both sides, and i sat there just thinking. Maybe it was meeting the Vietnam guy. And thinking about the Cong sneaking down the mountains at night. i realized that i wanted to hide out: from surveillance cameras and Internet watchers. That was why i had to lug this ROYAL up to the cabin and start using it where i <u>wouldn't</u> <u>be</u> <u>watched</u>. i'm gonna go back and underline that. There's a neat way to do that on this machine.

i would carry it up there if it took me all day. i could stop and rest on the stone walls. Probably nobody knew that path better than me.

i'd carry paper in my backpack. Fill up a pitcher with spring-water and go back in and start to type. Just to see what would come out.

i even decided to use a small i and not a capital I, so i could stay down, out of sight.

Don't get me wrong. i like computers. There's not much i haven't tried on a computer. i've done digital editing. i download some music. i like to check out webcams, i've played most of the games some of my school friends have. i've done some stuff i wish i hadn't.

But it's hard to shake the feeling that someone <u>in</u> there is watching me, tracking what i'm doing, writing, or thinking, 24/7. i know they do that. And even when i'm not online, just typing on a computer, i still feel connected to that whole world of plastic, electric circuitry, global corporations, shopping, advertising, pollution.

So if i go way off the grid and punch these antique keys up in a cabin somewhere, i'll be connected, but it'll be to a whole different world--a world that never went away--of iron and steel, mechanical type, printer's ink, paper, silence, the woods, water running in a stream. And no one's watching.

Or, at least, that was what i thought.

4

April 24

On Saturday, my whole family scattered. Dad went off to do some spring hiking with a few friends; Mom called it "male bonding." She and Claire were going for one of their two trips a year to the nearest mall, which is about forty miles away, in Massachusetts. They go once in the spring and once in the fall. All you out there in Malltown USA might find that hard to believe. Welcome to Vermont. They asked me to come, but i knew that the invitation was just a formality. They meant it to be a mom and daughter thing, and i was expected to give them a reason why i couldn't make it.

So i did. i said i had too much homework. That i was going to meet my posse at the Big Track Meet. i'd see them at dinner. Hey, could you pick up some Thai takeout for later?

By ten o'clock the house was totally quiet. i almost wanted to stay and hang out by myself. i like being alone there. But i had work to do. So i closed up and headed right back out to Franklin's barn on my bike.

It took me about two hours all told to get that old ROYAL up to Uncle Mo's cabin. It's at least half a mile through the woods. i bungeed the ROYAL back on the bike. For the first fifty yards, i would be in plain sight in the pasture, if anyone was watching. There were a few houses up the road, but there was no sign of life around them.

First i tried the bike in the woods, but it was hard going uphill over rough ground, so pretty soon i ditched the Vietcong act. i hid the bike in some bushes and carried the ROYAL by hand, with many stops. The thing was really heavy.

On the top of one steep part of the trail, the land to the left falls away like a cliff. There's an old hollow log there you can rest on and look down. The stream that runs by the cabin is below, and i was so tired i seriously considered lofting the machine into the air from the topmost point. Pictured it flying in slow motion like in a movie. Big crash when it hit. Watch it bounce on the rocks. See the cut glass break and sparkle in the sunlight.

But that would have been a cop-out, not to mention an ecological disaster. And then there was the thought i kept having that my whole trip had to be longer, and complete, not to mention exceedingly difficult, if it was going to be, like Miss Roth says, "transformative."

We made it to the cabin, eventually. ROYAL and me. Three steps up, and then along the side deck. i put it down where the deck met the front roofed porch.

"We're here," i told it. It said nothing. Like it was puzzled. Or afraid because we'd suddenly stopped. As long as it kept in some kind of motion, maybe extinction was only a bad dream.

i unlocked the door. "Unlock" here is a private joke. That means i slid the piece of old pine branch out of the iron ring that held the door closed. The cabin had never actually been locked in its life.

Mo once told me, "Vic, you lock a door way up here, somebody'd break in. Some hunter or stray kid. Smash a windowpane or a door hinge. This way, anyone who wants to can just come on in."

So, a few people had over the years. Once, someone had opened a can of beans and cooked it up on the woodstove. They left kind of a mess. Another time someone left a thankyou note on the table. "For the wonderful place to sit and think," something gushy like that.

Once I found that the bed had been used. Yeah, used.

But these break-ins were rare, and people always took the time to at least close the place back up and stick the pine branch back in the ring. i mean, hardly anyone knew where the cabin was. Even if you found it by accident, you'd have a hard time finding it again.

i opened a few windows near the table to let out the stale air. Got out the dustpan and broom and swept out the mouse turds. Took the Mexican bedspread off the sofa and shook it over the porch rails, holding my breath. You're not supposed to breathe mouse dust.

i climbed up to the sleeping loft and opened the windows there. It was a ritual i did every time i came up. i looked around for signs of visitors but didn't see any.

Then i brought the typewriter in and set it on the table.

"This better be good," i said out loud, "cause i'm not gonna carry you back down."

No answer.

"i mean, this is the end of the line. For you."

i let the ROYAL think about that for a while. Then i went out to the stream to fill my water bottle. First you have to clean out leaves and things and wait for the water in the stream to clear. Mo showed me where the best water was. "It's spring-fed along here," he said. "That about balances out any moose piss comin' down from uphill. Less risk of beaver fever." That's some stomach thing the soldiers used to get in Vietnam. He'd drink a whole jug just to show me it was okay.

The water was icy cold and sweet. i went back in with my full bottle and sat in front of the beautiful old keyboard. Set a stack of paper beside it.

Okay, i said, to myself and the machine. What about that story the guy said was in there? Again, no answer. i took a peek through the plate-glass window. Nothing but metal. What'd you expect, Victor?

i gazed around the cabin. i loved the insides of the logs, every one rough-shaped and different. All the windowsills were filled with dusty kids' toys, old board games, and stuff people brought back from their hikes: colorful stones, bracket funguses, beaver bones, birds' nests.

Coming through the window screens were some birdcalls i didn't know, and the sound of the little stream.

What a perfect place to hole up if i had to. Under the radar. It's not on the town list. There's this big tax map at the town clerk's where every single house has its little black dot. Uncle Mo's cabin's not even on it. He never applied for a building permit.

i was sure Mo would approve of what i was doing. Maybe i should just stay here for a while, i thought. Hide out. i pictured how i could live if i had to. Trapping small mammals, eating fiddleheads, sneaking to the edge of town at night to gather old food chucked out in back of the Price Chopper. Cook only at night, so no one would see the little plume of smoke. Type letters with no return address to friends, or to the newspaper, so people would know i was alive, and what i was thinking.

Finally i depressed the shift key with my left little finger and stretched over with my right forefinger, reaching for the letter A. That's not how they teach you to do it in keyboarding, but a one-handed capital A is the toughest move in typing, and i knew the ROYAL would require some strength. All that steel, all those springs. Not to mention the stiffness: i mean, the old guy said he'd oiled it, but what was it, thirty or forty years since anyone had actually used it? i hit the letter hard. And then kept on going.

When i finished for the day, i put the pages into my backpack and stuck a fresh sheet in the ROYAL. i liked how that looked, all ready for the first word the next time i came up to write.

i closed up, upstairs and downstairs. i always put stuff away and then stand in the doorway for a minute to check, because part of the ritual is to leave the place looking like no one has been there.

Of course, now, anyone coming in after me would say, Hey, that thing wasn't there before. Not that anyone would. Come after me, i mean.

No heavy load now. i hiked back fast, got my bike out of the bushes, and pedaled hard down the last bit of trail, skidding in places, or catching some air. Aimed right at the roots and

stones so i could feel the jolts hit my body. i shot out of the
trees and through the break in the stone wall--there's a hump
just before it that gets you flying. i landed just right. Then i
bounced through Franklin's back field and headed home.

We were eating Thai noodles and sesame chicken with a
sweet-and-sour sauce when my mom asked, "What did you do
today?"

i told her about the cabin but not about the ROYAL.

"You really love that place, don't you?" she said.

"Yes."

"I don't," Claire said, slurping up a long noodle. "There's
nothing to do there."

My mom looked at her like she was realizing all the work
she still had to do on Claire.

"We should all go out there sometime soon," she said. "Take
care of it for Mo."

"The cabin's fine, Mom," i said. "i cleaned it all out. Nobody's been there all winter."

"I keep thinking he should sell it," she said. "But then we
wouldn't have it to use."

"Nobody'd want it, Mom. You can't drive there. There's no
plumbing or electricity or anything."

"A hunter might," she said. "They don't mind hiking in."

i didn't like that. i'm not against hunting, but i don't want
the cabin to change into a camp where four or five guys sit
around oiling their guns, and drink beer and smoke and tell
dirty jokes, take long pisses off the porch, then get up at dawn
to go out and kill deer.

"Well, keep that idea to yourself, please," i told her, "at least till i'm out of high school."

"What do you like so much about the place?" she asked.

"i can think there."

i said that on purpose cause i knew that would end this part of our conversation. All my life she'd been encouraging me to "develop an inner life" (her words), putting me in my room when i was little till i decided to change my mood, showing me all her books and getting me to read, but then turning my bedroom light out before i was really sleepy, so i'd have time to just think.

i wanted her to picture me purposely trekking out to her brother's cabin deep in the woods to do a spell of Thinking. Doing the Thoreau thing. i knew she would approve of that and stay out of my way. Then we talked some about the woods in spring and her old commune. That's when i said casually, Hey, what was the name of that commune book i liked? With the nice drawings? Do you know where it is? i might want to write about it, for English class maybe--which wasn't <u>exactly</u> true but wasn't a lie, either.

i certainly wouldn't tell her or anyone else the real reason i wanted that book.

5

April 29

Sometimes things jump into your life and push everything else to the side. All i could think of was, i want to get back up to the cabin. Halfway through the week i realized that i didn't have to wait till Saturday. It was springtime in Vermont, and most of the students and teachers had this unspoken agreement that homework was no longer the Big Important Thing it used to be in November.

Thursday afternoon i rode out directly from school. i turned in by Franklin's barn and hit the pasture. This time i kept going all the way up to the cabin.

Have you ever been in the woods in New England in late April? It's amazing. You can't help but notice all the signs that spring has really started. i love all the streams, and how everything seems so much purer than in summer and fall, because there are no big leaves to block sight or sound. There's lots of green around you and above you, but it's all fresh and pale, like it's just starting out.

i opened the log cabin, then checked to see if anyone had been there--that was the first thing i always checked out. i

didn't feel like eating the snacks i had brought. It felt like food
from a world i'd left behind, so i went out and got fresh water
and ate a few peanuts from an old can on the shelf. Freezing
and thawing hadn't helped their taste.

Then i took my finished pages out of my backpack.

And the book from my mom's bookshelf. i took that out,
too.

My mom is an ex-hippie, meaning she used to live on a farm
commune around here. She'll tell me about it if i ask her--
about most of it, anyway--but i usually don't ask her. For one
thing, it's embarrassing to think of her doing the stuff she
talks about. (It's even more embarrassing for my dad, who
wasn't there.) For another thing, i already know a lot about it,
cause i've read all her books on the subject.

She collects books on the commune movement--she thinks
we need to remember how to do it, you know, to get away
from money and war and go mess around with cows, tractors,
big organic gardens, just in case land gets cheap again.

The book in my hands was a novel. It was set on another
farm that used to be near the cabin. The man who wrote it did
the pen and ink drawings, too.

One of the pictures is of a skinny guy with long hair, in a
pretty decrepit farmhouse room. He's standing beside a
woodstove and a desk with a typewriter. You can see through
the window that it's nighttime. On the desk there's an old
lamp made out of a duck decoy. The guy is smiling, holding a
metal coffeepot in his left hand, with steam coming out of it.

But here's the thing: the guy is totally naked. You can see
everything. All he has on is a pair of wire-rim glasses. The caption of the picture says, "You have to be naked to write."

The drawing was the reason i had brought the book out there in my pack. i sat there looking at it.

Don't get the wrong idea. It's just that i always wondered what the caption meant.

"You have to be naked to write."

It was like one of those logic puzzles. Just a couple of clues and you have to figure out the rest. Did it mean that you have to strip your heart or soul totally bare in order to come out with the truth? Let go of everything you're used to, if you really want to know yourself?

Or get rid of any outward sign of your century if you want to write for real?

There was only one way to find out.

i started with my running shoes, and then my socks and sweatshirt. That wasn't hard, but it was a moment or two before i could get on with the rest. i kept looking out the windows, kept imagining voices in the sound the water made. You get water and stones together a certain way and it's like a little crowd of people clinking glasses and making conversation in the next room. You can almost understand what they're saying. They're talking about you.

i was wondering what my dad or mom or Claire would say if they saw me. If they thought i was a little strange before, which i knew they did, this would prove it.

Jeans next, T-shirt.

i looked around again. Finish the job, man, i told myself.

Underpants.

i put all the clothes in a pile--just a few steps to my right in case i had to grab them quickly. i couldn't see myself. There wasn't a mirror in the whole cabin. Not that i would have looked if there was.

How i felt: freed in a way, vulnerable, also alive to the breeze coming in the window right in front of me. Right away i had goose bumps on my upper arms and the fronts of my thighs. It was almost May, not really hot weather yet. And inside the cabin was always chillier than outside, except in the dead of winter with the fire going.

This is probably the first time i've been completely naked anywhere besides my own house, i thought.

Part of me sort of shrank, if you know what i mean. i started to shiver but i took a couple of deep breaths and that stopped it.

The chair seat was cold. And the back. i sat there for a moment and didn't move. Then, with a new piece of paper, i leaned forward and started to write. Let's see if this works, i thought.

Pretty soon it seemed like the caption under the picture had it right.

It was like from the moment i spotted the typewriter in the yard sale, my whole life had been taken over by some kind of secret knowledge. The picture caption was another part of that knowledge. It was like there's this other universe out there, waiting for me to access it, but there's a couple of simple steps--well, actually, not simple at all--that i have to take to get there. Then, once i'm there--

The words just started to pour out of me. Like something had been in the way, and now it was gone. i could hardly type fast enough to keep up. The ROYAL shook, and it made all its great sounds like the last time but faster--the rub of the hard rubber roller, the keys clicking, the letters swinging up and back, the type slamming against the paper, the thump of the space bar, the bell at the end of each typed line like the bell in a boxing match. Round's over, back to your corner. Then even those sounds just faded out.

Five or six times or more, the only thing i was aware of was changing the paper. You have to do that with typewriters. Filled-up page out, new blank one in. Feed it in straight if you want it to look right. i'm not saying that what i was writing was great or earthshaking. That's not the point.

Have you ever been writing something when you just forgot where you were, and what time it was, and you kept diving down deeper into your words?

No, it's more like diving down through your words--past them, and way further down into someplace else.

In fact, it doesn't matter whether you're naked or not, since the next thing is, you leave your body totally behind and just go off into your mind. A whole other part of your mind.

All i know is i was so deep into it, that caption was so right, that i never heard a sound from outside, not even the breaking of a twig.

So it must have been some other sense, maybe a shiver on the back of my neck, that made me whip my head around and see the face at the window.

6

i jumped up. Never moved so fast in my life! Grabbed my pants and my running shoes, nothing else, and i was hurling my legs into the pants and my bare feet into the shoes all at once as i ran out the door. i don't know why i didn't holler, or hide. i wasn't afraid. Just hugely pissed off.

In less than ten seconds, i hit the porch, tripped on one half-on sneaker and nearly fell, then turned and ran to the back side of the house--

She was nowhere to be seen.

Yeah, she. She. SHE.

i couldn't hear her running, or breathing hard, or snapping branches, nothing. i had absolutely no idea which direction she'd gone.

i picked a direction, plunged uphill to the main path. Tried to cut her off near the outhouse, but there were no signs, no stomped-on ferns, nothing, and it was a mess in there--with six-foot blackberry shoots everywhere. Thorns! i was getting scratched all over my bare chest and sides. Wrong way.

How could she vanish so fast?

Is she a ghost? i thought. But the cabin's not old enough to have a ghost. Or maybe she moves superhuman fast, like that goddess with wings on her sandals--no, that was a god who did that, i thought, but speaking of gods and goddesses, it's like one of those Latin poems where women trying to get away change really quickly--that's it, she metaphormo, i mean meta_mor_phosed into a tree, and if i had gotten out there quicker, hadn't tripped on my sneaker, i'd have seen it happen. i looked around, in a 360. Everything was quiet.

Something made me keep my mouth shut.

i went back inside, stamping my feet on the steps in case she was under the porch listening. i put the rest of my clothes on and sat back in my chair. Stared at the typewriter.

Didn't feel like writing anymore. i thought, i'll just sit here and listen to my heart pound. Catch my breath. One thing i knew: the cabin would never, that's never, be the same for me again.

i must have sat there for half an hour. i was afraid to move. i never did turn around. i knew she wasn't there. Nothing else was going to happen. And if she was there, i was not going to give her the pleasure of seeing me look back at her again.

The sun got lower, and finally there was nothing i could do except add all the pages i'd just typed to the pile. i slipped them underneath to keep the order right. i put them in my pack, left a fresh sheet in the ROYAL, closed the cabin, picked up my bike, and headed out of the woods.

i rode fast back down the trail, too fast--almost wiped out on the steep part.

Funny, i had never paid much attention to the houses near the Franklin place. Now i came out at the bottom of the trail, rode around the barn and house, and stopped where the driveway meets the road. There were four or five houses within sight. Not right there, but close enough: slightly uphill, all in a crooked row across the street.

They all needed paint and tree pruning and trips to the dump. i had no real reason to suspect any of them, but now i wondered if in one of those houses there was a girl pulling back a curtain or a blind, watching me. From the inside now. Maybe i should ride up and see--

i headed home.

i said i don't like to be noticed. It's my big issue, i guess you could say. Thinking about going under the radar came naturally to me.

i have a few friends. We hang out in school and sometimes downtown, but i don't usually make much of an effort to get together with anyone. i'd really rather be alone, with my bike or Will's books. My mom and dad got concerned about that. They went to see a family therapist to ask if that was normal. Course my mom couldn't keep it to herself. To hear her tell it, the therapist used one of those caterpillar-cocoon-butterfly metaphors, said soon enough i'd be multicolored, fine, flying away on my own, and not to worry.

Good for my self-esteem, to be compared to a weightless insect flitting among the flowers. Eating pollen.

If they'd asked me, i could have told them. It's like i'm still in my trying-to-figure-it-all-out phase, and until i've got it figured out, i'd rather not be the object of attention. From anybody.

Now, i had just been more noticed than i'd ever been in my life. i felt like my embarrassment ought to show on me somewhere. All the drivers passing me, why weren't they honking their horns, grinning and waving to each other, pointing me out--there he is, that's the guy!

i went over what happened back at the cabin.

i focused on that half second after i turned around and saw her looking, just looking, before either of us moved. i didn't have time to think then, but i did now. And i was pretty certain of a few things.

Number one, i didn't recognize her.

Two, she wasn't judging; she was just, you know, an observer.

Three, she was friendly. You don't smile the way she did and not be friendly.

Four, she wasn't going to run right out and tell someone. How did i know that? i didn't <u>know</u> it, i just felt it. i could still see her face in my mind, her expression, and it was saying, Well, this is an interesting scene: I wonder what <u>that</u> feels like.

What all this added up to at that moment was that i suddenly realized something totally unexpected. It almost knocked me off my bike.

i didn't mind her seeing me. i, who don't like to be noticed. i didn't mind being seen.

7

We ate early that night. i sat there with my back and neck clenched, dreading the dinner table conversation. There was no way i would say anything about the cabin.

i mean, how would this sound?

"Hey, funny thing happened today. i was sitting stark naked up at Mo's cabin--you know, like in the picture in that commune book? And some girl spied on me. Can you believe? Any idea how i can find out who she is? i'd like to meet her."

Uh-uh.

Just eat, i told myself, answer questions, compliment the cooking, try to be nice to Claire, help clean up, and get out.

My first mouthful, i bit my tongue hard. i was that tense.

In between his chews, my dad asked, "How was your day, Vic?"

i don't like to be called Vic, but with your family you don't have much choice.

"Okay."

"School going all right?"

"Yeah."

"What did you do after school?"

"Oh, i went up to the cabin." i tried to make it sound totally casual. Like i'd almost forgotten where i'd been and what i'd done.

"You working on anything?" my mom asked. This is her most frequent, go-to question. She figures all spare time is idle time unless you're working on something arty. She's a throwback. She should have been a pioneer wife, making quilts and pies and braiding rugs and sewing all of Claire's little cotton dresses. That's what she used to do, actually, in her hippie days. A long time ago she looked me in the eye and decided i was the same way. If i ever complained of boredom, she was always "Go whittle some wood. Go draw something."

So "you working on anything?" is her way of checking up on me, to make sure i don't take any detours from my personal journey of self-understanding through art. That's one reason. The other one is that she believes that making art is the most therapeutic activity ever known to humanity; so as long as i'm engaged in something creative, my mental health has got to be okay. i won't be tripping out on some illegal herb or chemical, like she used to do back in the day.

"Yeah, actually, i'm writing a story," i said, "a long one." i held up both hands as if displaying a large imaginary fish i'd almost caught. i was thinking, Don't ask, don't ask--

"What's it about?" Claire asked. Showing a rare flash of interest.

"Not much," i said.

But she wouldn't let it go. "Come on. Tell us."

"No way!" i said, too loud and too quick.

She looked right back down at her food.

Uh-oh, i thought, don't be so touchy, Victor. Calm down. You're going to give yourself away. After that, all my answers seemed to do what i hoped. To satisfy my mom and dad. Close off further questioning with just a little mystery. i felt pretty good.

i was flying under the family radar.

After dinner i went up to sit in Will's room. i needed to think about what had happened.

No one ever bothers me in there. When the door is closed, that means my privacy has to be respected, like Will's always was. Rooms in our house are like that, after you reach a certain age. Course, with my own room it's harder, cause the door doesn't really close tight. It's an old house, a little tippy at one end. If i want my door to stay closed, i stick a sock or something between it and the jamb or whatever it's called.

So, in Will's room, with the tighter door, if i wanted to, i could go right to the secret place behind his sweater drawer where he keeps a few magazines i probably shouldn't be looking at. i could look at the pictures.

i thought, Maybe if i take a look at a picture, it will help me sort out how i feel--yeah, i'll do that. But right away i thought, No, that's twisted, it's just an excuse. Halfway to the dresser in the closet, i slung myself into the easy chair instead and picked up a book. The pictures could wait.

But it was hard to read. Sometimes in the course of a day, exciting things happen, and you get all this energy built up and stuck inside you, and you have to do something with it--

Anyway, it was a good thing i started flipping through <u>Ishi</u> instead of a magazine, cause there was a knock on the door, kind of quiet.

"Come in."

It was Claire. She shut the door after her. She had never come into Will's room while i was in there. But as soon as she walked in, it felt right.

i think family houses have invisible boundaries in them. They get drawn, then everyone begins to see them, to respect them. After dinner and chores, in our house anyway, my parents retreat to their side of the boundary. i rarely go over there at night. They have parent stuff to do, or things they want to read or watch or talk about, and i head up to where my homework is, or to my books. What i'm getting at here is that it should have been natural for Claire to hang out nearer to me. But i don't think i'd ever given it a thought. i don't think i ever noticed what she actually did after dinner.

Hey, it wasn't my fault, or hers, that our parents didn't decide until five or six years after i was born to have another kid. To me, she was like from another planet. If they had wanted a close relationship between us, it didn't make sense for them to wait that long. Parents ought to think about stuff like that. But maybe it wasn't a thought-out decision, maybe she just, you know, happened.

But there she was in Will's room with me. She had this testing look on her face that said, "I'm gonna give you this one chance."

She climbed up into the big chair with me, i'm glad she's not too old to do that. i made room for her so she could squeeze in next to me. She just sat there like that for a minute. She's always wearing her soccer clothes. Even her shin guards. She sheds bits of dried grass wherever she goes. She plays defense, she likes to slide-tackle, get dirty.

i put my arm around her shoulder. She's still pretty small and skinny. She cut her hair recently for the first time ever, and now it's too short to braid but too long for styling. It's hair still figuring out what to do.

Then she turned to look at me. "You hurt my feelings," she said, and the minute she said it i knew why.

"i'm sorry," i said. i meant it.

"You know how?" she asked.

"Yeah. You asked a question and i blew it off."

She nodded. She was right, a sister deserves more explanation. Maybe not the whole explanation, but enough to get a little conspiracy going.

So i told her some of it. i said i was writing--practicing writing actually, on an old typewriter up at Mo's, and it was mostly, i don't know, nature stuff, family history, stream of consciousness--i had to tell her what that meant. It didn't have a title or a plot yet, so there wasn't much to report. i let all that out but no more, and i sat there hoping it was enough.

It was. i mean she probably only wanted me to acknowledge that she existed. That i could trust her. That we could be friends.

"What are you reading?" she asked. Whew, subject changed.

"Ishi. It's an anthropology book, but it's just about my favorite story."

"What's it about?"

"It's about the last 'Stone Age' Indian found living in the United States. It's a true story. i don't know why but it really gets me."

Then i suddenly realized. Ishi was the original under-the-radar guy. See, if Claire hadn't come in just then and asked me, i probably would never have noticed. Things happen for a reason.

In 1911 there was no radar to fly under. Well, bats had radar, but people didn't. But there was a railroad not far from Ishi's hideout, in northern California. And white men--hikers, hunters, and surveyors--walked right by Ishi where he was hiding and holding his breath in the bushes. He was sure they would kill him if they saw him. With their fire sticks. They never knew he was there. They found his lean-to and took his bow and arrows and his water basket, thinking they were ancient relics. He just about starved after that. He and the last few members of his whole tribe.

i was telling all this to Claire. When you have a favorite story, you may as well practice telling it. Maybe knowing how to tell it could come in handy someday.

Now, see, that's obviously a thought i never would have had before getting the ROYAL. i keep getting these little rushes, like those messages i mentioned before. How do i know this stuff all of a sudden? Did the guy know the ROYAL was going to wake up that unused part of my brain? Was that what his smile was all about?

"So what happened next?" Claire was asking.

"Well, his cousin died, she was a woman about his age i think and they loved each other, like you and i do, you know, like brother and sister. And then his mother died. He almost

went crazy because he was all alone, the last of his tribe. He
didn't have anybody to talk to. He hibernated, i think he slept
in a grizzly bear's cave. In the spring he burned off his hair in
mourning--"

"What's that?"

"That's when someone you love dies and you act different
and dress different and pray a lot for their spirit, you make
yourself look as miserable as you feel, that's why you burn off
your hair--"

"Wow."

i could tell she was liking the story, so i told her more of it,
about what happened when Ishi made it to the land of the
white people. Then finally she'd heard enough and said, "I really only came in to say good night."

"G'night," i said, and hugged her. And that was that.

She got down off the chair and crossed the room, dropping
bits of grass. i realized that from then on she would knock and
come in when she wanted. She was choosing our side of the
boundary. Our territory. And that was okay.

She closed the door carefully.

i looked at it, but i was thinking about the window, and the
face. That girl had come out of nowhere. We lived in a small
town. She must have been under the radar, too.

8

April 30

In school on Friday i spent the whole time finding any excuse i could to look everywhere: in the halls, in the caf, the gym, the learning center, everywhere. i wanted to look at every girl's face. But in my heart i already knew she wasn't there. i knew, if she was, i would feel it.

We have one high school. It's bigger than our town needs, but that's because all the smaller towns within ten miles send their students there. Still, it's not that big. If i couldn't find her, there was a reason. Maybe she was absent. Absent a lot. Or maybe she had already graduated and just looked younger, or maybe she went to some prep school and just happened to be home right now. Maybe she was here visiting someone. Or maybe she lived here but she homeschooled.

As school ended, i spun the imaginary needle on the dial in my brain, and it landed on that. Homeschooled it was. What Mr. Crockett, my geometry teacher, calls a "working hypothesis."

Then i started working with it. If she's homeschooled, i thought, she could be sheltered like some really religious people are, but i didn't think so. She was way up in the woods, and she disappeared really quickly when i chased her. Most Vermonters who homeschool spend a lot of time outside, studying nature. That's one of the main reasons that parents keep their kids out of school. i'm with them on that. Most months, spring and fall, i feel like a prisoner inside those concrete walls.

While i was riding home from school, it was like her personality began to take shape behind the face i had seen so briefly. Then i stopped short—if she <u>was</u> homeschooled, would she have gone back to the cabin? Right then, while I was looking for her in school? She could be <u>in</u> the cabin right now—

i wanted to rush up there, but Mom had my afternoon programmed with a dentist appointment and yard work. i coasted into our driveway and looked in the general direction of Mo's cabin, trying to see her through three neighborhoods, two hills, and about ten thousand trees, trying to picture whether she was there or not. But i'd have to wait to find out.

Thinking about tomorrow, about Saturday, reminded me of the old yard sale guy on the top of Greenleaf Street. i could imagine him a month ago fixing up the ROYAL in his workshop. Listening to some country music station. It's always some guy moaning about a woman who left him, or a dog or a guardian angel or a gallon of beer. Typewriter man's got a shop apron and safety glasses on, and bottles of cleaning liquids. He's leaning over the machine with his toothbrush, chuckling to himself about his little secret, what this old ROYAL's going to do for the person he decides to give it to.

9

May 1

We're supposed to go on a family trip.

Mom works at a bookstore. She has to work a half day on Saturday, so i figure i have two or three hours. If she's surprised at my heading out so early, she doesn't show it.

She's getting ready for work. We have an old mirror by our kitchen door. She does this funny thing with mirrors, she turns her head partway to the left and sucks in her cheeks. i think she wishes her cheekbones showed, or maybe she thinks if she keeps looking and sucking enough, they'll pop out all of a sudden.

"We're leaving at two, Victor," she tells me. With her head turned and her cheeks sucked in. But her eyes are on me, reflected in the glass.

i'm wolfing down cereal. "i'll be back about one."

i ride as hard as i can. Should i try to get there a different way? i mean, try to make it into the woods without what's-her-name seeing me? Will she be watching? What do i want? Do i want her to see me and follow? Or do i want to tiptoe up to the cabin on the chance that she's already in there and sur-

prise <u>her</u>? But then i get one of those instructions in my head
--telling me to change nothing, to do everything exactly as i
did it before.

Right, i reply, good advice. Just ride to the cabin, park your
bike, open the door, yank off all your clothes, sit down, and
wait for her to show up. What, are you crazy?

So i ride in plain sight across the pasture. Trying to sense
whether anyone's watching from the houses up the road.
Can't tell. Pedal up the trail, breathing hard. i don't meet her.
That would be too easy. i make the last turn by the ferny place
and down toward the little waterfall--and when i say "little" i
mean little. It's only about six inches wide. Makes plenty of
noise, though; something about the shape of the rock basin it
splashes into--

i stop. No clear view inside from where i'm standing. Don't
sneak up, i decide. Too much like peeping. i leave the bike off
the trail behind a bush. Climb the three steps, slowly and with
more noise than usual, just to warn her, if she's in there.

My heart's pounding. Stare straight ahead, don't look
through the deck window. But when i'm on the porch, i see
right away that the door is still locked. The old pine branch
stuck in its place.

She's not here.

Nothing in the cabin looks disturbed. No footprints. Typewriter, pile of fresh blank paper an arm's length beyond it. i sort
of sneak up on the ROYAL as if i can surprise it, maybe find a
message typed there on the paper i left loaded. But nothing.

i sit down. Throw a look over my shoulder to check out the
window. Still nothing. i turn back.

That's when i notice the blue jay feather on the top sheet of the blank paper stack. When i pick it up, this is what i see written underneath:

I've read that book, too.

Slap.

All right. This is a game, i think. i do games. She wants to play, i can play.

i sit on the edge of the chair. i keep my clothes on. i'm not about to write anything now. We're on to something else. There's another logic problem to solve first. Well, more like a detective thing, interpreting the clues.

I've read that book, too.

What i know:

She was in here. Duh.

She wrote with a pen. There's nothing in the cabin that can write like that. So she must have brought her own pen with her. She must have had a reason to. Maybe she came to write.

She's not here now. Wait, i think; check that one out. I climb partway up the sleeping-loft ladder and poke my head through the hole. Nobody upstairs. Look in the tool closet. Nobody.

What does a feather mean? Birds, nature, flying, lightness-- tickling! She likes to play games, or jokes. She has a sense of humor.

That's what i know. All i know. Here's what i think:

She's been to the cabin before.

How do i know that? i <u>don't</u>; i just said, i <u>think</u> it. The fact that when i just came in i saw no sign of her here means that there could have been lots of other times when she was here

and left no sign. What <u>could</u> have been probably was. Just because, as a general rule, what <u>could</u> be probably <u>is</u>.

Add to that the fact that she seems to be a woods person. i
can picture her discovering this cabin on her own. Maybe a
long time ago. Maybe it's her cabin like it is mine, although i
never knew it, because she never leaves any sign.

What other logical leaps can i take?

Whether she goes to school or studies at home, she's read
the book with that picture in it. Wait. That's not just a logical
leap, that's one thing i <u>know</u>. That means she reads adult
books. She's a woods person. She reads the same kinds of
books i read, and she had that look on her face. We're similar.
So, i'm betting she's not from a wacko cult that keeps her out
of school for some religious or political reason. <u>If</u> she doesn't
go to school. That's still an if.

i can picture her clearly, leaving her house. Down the porch
steps of one of those houses across from Franklin's. She turns
downhill, to the right. She sees the sunlight hit a shiny blue
feather in the grass. She stops and picks it up. Decides to keep
it. She holds it in her fingers as she crosses the road, the field,
then puts it behind her ear for the walk up through the
woods. You put them in from behind, pointy end first. Pull
them through a little so they stay put.

Her right ear. She's probably right-handed. First of all, because most people are. Second of all, from the way the feather
was lying on the paper, quill slanting down to the right,
feather end up left. i see her reach up to her right ear, carefully
pull the feather through and out and lower it and place it over
the words she just wrote. Smiling.

When did this happen?

Probably not today. Why not? Cause there hasn't been enough "today" yet. It's still early. She must have been here yesterday, just like i thought. That means she hasn't been here yet today! Which means if she is half as anxious to actually meet me as i am to meet her, she's on her way right now!

Another logical leap. Two leaps, actually, two more possibilities:

One: she didn't see me ride by, and she's just coming up on her own time. If she's coming up on her own time, she could be planning to surprise me by <u>being</u> here when i get here. That means she could be getting here very soon.

To the cabin?

Into the cabin?

To do what i was doing? Oh my god--

She said she's read the book, which meant she's seen the picture. Was that a hint? If i weren't already here in the cabin when she got here, would she, you know, and wonder whether i'd look in the window and see her the way she saw me? Then i think, That <u>is</u> <u>exactly</u> what the feather and the five words meant-- Wait, no, she wanted me to get here first and find the feather: it was her way of telling me that i had already missed my chance to see her. That she had already sat here like that, writing. Like me. All her clothes folded next to her. All of them! No, not folded. Just tossed on the floor. Yeah, tossed. Girls do that. Maybe yesterday. Yes yesterday! i couldn't believe it! When i was looking for her in school, she was here nake--

Wait--second possibility: let's say she did see me ride by just now. Say we take that as fact, a given. We know she's observant. She probably was waiting with a view of Franklin's drive-way. Up in one of those houses. Curtains parted just a bit. If so, that means she's on her way now. Probably taking it slow to give me time to see the note, think about it, and decide what to do. Or just making me wait. Either way, it's another game. She likes games. Either way, i got here first, and she's almost here! She's probably just hitting the clearing now--

i mean, as soon as i think that, i hit the floor. i dive off the chair and come up hurtling on all fours toward the back window. i stay low. Crawling at top speed. i'm amazed how quickly i'm breathing. It's as if she is deep inside my mind, controlling my reactions, controlling everything, with almost no effort on her part, and no hurry.

i lean my back against the logs under the window. Now i'm facing the door. Course i can't surprise her because the door is open. No way to lock the place from the inside. When she turns the corner, we'll both see each other at the same time. No, i'll hear her footsteps on the porch. No, she'll be tiptoe-ing. No she won't. Yes she will, because she knows i got there first. No, she may not know. That was a given, but i knew it wasn't guaranteed; it was just for the sake of logic. That's the trouble with calling something a given if it's really only a hypothesis. If she didn't see me, she may not know, she may be-- i can still--

As quick as i can, i wheel around, reach up and grab the windowsill, and haul myself up just high enough to see out. There she is! Morning sunlight in her face, halfway across the clearing. Still fifty feet away. Her and her dog.

Then i act without thinking. i drop. i shoot across the floor, still crawling, and hit the sleeping-loft ladder. Even if she glanced through the window, she wouldn't see me do that--it's out of her sight line. i'm up it in about two seconds. i throw myself through the hole at the top and lie on the floor of the loft breathing hard.

There's a thick round log along the whole edge of the loft. You can't see up over it from the floor below. Of course, now i'm trapped. And i can't see down. No way out. Damn. Now that i have a moment to think, i wish i had walked out the door and met her on the steps. Invited her in. Pleased to meet you. You want a drink of water?

Should have done that when i had the chance. Too late now.

i hear her scuffing along the deck. Hear her hesitate when she sees the door already open. Did i say there is a screen door? There is. i hear her, hear her actual voice, for the first time:

"Stay out here, Dash." i hear a low whine from the dog, and then i hear the clicking of uncut dog toenails on the wood decking, and the squeak of the screen door hinge as she comes in. No slam. She must be closing it carefully. Listening.

i'm lying frozen in place. Not daring to breathe. She doesn't say anything. i hear her step to the table. i can't see her but i know exactly what she's doing. She must see my backpack right there. On the floor next to the chair. Damn. Don't look in it. I hear her pick it up and put it down. She's puzzled. She's seeing the feather where i moved it off her message. i hear a chair scrape. Some rustling. Is she taking her backpack off? Oh, god.

What is she thinking? That i've gone out to the spring or the outhouse? That i'm hiding somewhere, waiting for her, waiting to spy on her? Good guess! That's exactly what i'm doing. But her dog would have found me by now if i were out there. She must know that.

Maybe not.

How long does she think i'll be gone? Is she going to write? With her pen? More rustling. A door opens and closes. The tool closet. Silence. Did she go in there to look for me? To hide? To take her clothes off? Am i crazy? Yes. Is she crazy? i don't know. i don't know her! Silence for longer than i can stand. Is she standing totally still? How can she not hear my breathing? My heart thumping? i'm supposed to be home in an hour!

Home. If i were any kind of normal teenage boy, home is exactly where i'd be, sleeping late on Saturday morning, till i'm yanked out of bed by my mom or dad ten minutes before we're supposed to leave for wherever we're going, or maybe if i happened to have gotten up early i'd be in my room, curtains closed--i don't even have any curtains--playing some video game, working on my thumb muscles, my vacant stare, my pale complexion.

But no. That kind of normal stuff never occurs to me, instead i go picking through yard sales, grab weird old typewriters, and look what happens to me, here i am, totally trapped in a cabin a mile from the closest human being-- No, there's one dangerous human being very close, and she has me trapped, she knew i was here, she spied on me, stalked me, she could be some kind of sexual predator, she's probably naked or getting naked three feet down from where i'm lying. i shouldn't be here, this is her territory, i thought it was mine, but i was so wrong-- i can't move a muscle, i have nothing to protect myself with, and if i bolt and rush the ladder, hit the floor and run toward the door, she'll trip me up and jump me, or if i get by her, her guard dog will bury his teeth in my leg, i'll fall and hit my head on the porch rail, maybe get killed--

"Victor?"

Oh my god.

How does she know my name?

You know how when you're playing hide-and-seek, you hear your name called, and you can tell by the angle of the sound that it's aimed right at you, they found out right where you are, no matter how good you thought your hiding place was?

"Are you gonna come down, or should I come up?"

My mind races. Wait a minute; are these the only two possible choices? Surely there must be more, like, couldn't i just lie still and pretend i'm not here? Maybe she would miraculously <u>not</u> come up the ladder, just do whatever it is she came here to do, take as long as she needs, i wouldn't watch, and then she would leave? Or, better still, she and her dog could head back down the trail right now. Or: she could shut her eyes and let <u>me</u> slip out of the cabin. Dog shut his eyes too. None of those seems actually reasonable, though, so i have to admit she has pretty much summed up the options available to both of us at the moment. It's on me. i have to answer. Still flat on my back but trying to sound casual, mature:

"i guess i'll come down."

i absolutely do not recognize the sound of my own voice. Sounds like it's coming from a distance. From a frog one pond over.

"Okay," she says.

"Or you could come up."

"You're just repeating what I said!" Her voice rises a little, irritated. i'm clearly stalling. Which makes her wonder.

"Are you alone?" she asks.

"Yes," i croak. But i liked that she thought that thought.

"So, should I come up? Are girls allowed?"

Where do you mean? i think. Upstairs? In the whole cabin? In my life?

"Are you decent?" i ask. My mom always says that. It's kind of a family joke, like when you're knocking on a bedroom door.

Then, right away, i wish i could take that question back. i wish it more than i've ever wished for anything in my whole life. If i had handed her my brain on a platter, with a diagram and a set of dissection tools, i couldn't have given her a clearer view into how my mind works.

She laughs quick, loud, hard, and surprised. Almost a snort.

"Of course I'm decent!"

Then i hear her clomp on the first step. Clomp on the second. She's made the decision for us.

i called it a ladder but it's built out of big split logs--it's as much a stairway as a ladder. It's seven steps that lead up to a three-foot-square hole in the loft floor. You can fit a body through the hole, or a little chair, but not a mattress or a blanket chest. Those came up over the log next to where i'm lying. This hole is about two feet from where my head is, on the floor. The rest of my body, too. i'm lying on my back. As i hear her come up, i just have time to twist my neck and head to the left. Then i'm looking right into her face as it pokes up through the hole.

Third time's a charm, i think. First time i saw that face i had craned my head over my naked shoulder and there it was slanted at the window's edge. Second time, a few minutes ago, i'd leaped my head up and right back down and caught a quick picture of it like a trout nabbing a fly. Now here we are, and it --her face--is really close, but we have a geometric problem. My body is horizontal and hers is vertical. So, my eyes are vertical and hers are horizontal.

She's the first one to adjust. She leans her head way over to the right side to line up our eyes. Like tracing paper. When you get the image below to line up with the one on top.

So. Her head is now almost lying on the floor, too.

This is what i see: she has skin that looks "disgustingly healthy." That's our family doctor's favorite expression. Like you cheated him out of a high-paying repair job. She looks like she rarely goes indoors. She has curly brown hair. "Curly" doesn't do it justice. It looks like it would break a comb, so combs never go there. Or scissors. Really wide brown eyes, friendly. Upward-slanting smile tracks at the corners of her lips. She smiles without showing teeth. Takes practice.

She has pierced ears, two or three little gold hoops going up each ear. Two necklaces of colored stones i'll bet you could see through if you held them up to the light. i can see two T-shirts, at least the very tops of them, one over the other. The one closest to her skin is faded orange and frayed. The one on top is newer, bright red, wider at the neck. Like when one fades you don't take it off. You leave it there and put a new one over it. That's as far down as i can see. The rest is still standing on the ladder.

i have the strangest feeling i've ever had. When i say "feeling" i mean like what your five senses tell you. i feel like up till that moment i've been experiencing a low-level chill. Not for that long, a little over sixteen years. And now, where this chill was, i'm feeling something else. Warmth, radiating right out of her.

All this is taking place in about three seconds, maybe four, while at the same time i'm mentally flipping through all the possible cool ways i could introduce myself. How have i done it in the past? Lots of ways. Would any of those work here? i dismiss every idea as incredibly stupid--

Hello my name is Victor oh you already know that do you come here often ahhhh so finally we meet who are you what are you doing here why are you following me have we ever met before? welcome to my uncle Mo's cabin did you know he built it when he came home crazy from Vietnam? i'm the only one who ever comes here well that is except you, i mean i think you must come here a lot maybe even more than me i can't believe you saw me naked i'm glad i wasn't doing anything well i was doing something i was just writing but you know what i mean oh shit i absolutely can't say that! oh god were you really here yesterday just like in the picture in the book? you were weren't you, that's what the note meant, i wish i had seen you no i don't really mean that, well i actually do, but what i really mean is:

"Hi."

"Hi, Victor." Her smile gets bigger. There goes my introduction.

"How do you know my name?"

"It's on the backpack downstairs. Isn't that your backpack?"

"Oh, yeah. i must have put my name on it."

"It's right on the label."

"The label?"

"In the little plastic window."

Well now that's just fine. Damn. Some young idiot wants to go under the radar then walks around with his name on his backpack. And his address. She being a spy, she's memorized it already and now she can sneak to my house and peep at me through <u>that</u> window. i'm never gonna be able to get away with anything. What about my privacy? i'll go home and say Mom you've got to sew me some curtains. Like right away. Do you have any cloth? Let's go buy some. No, Mom, i can't tell you why. Fine, i'll get Dad to do it.

"So," she says.

"So what?" i say.

"Are you gonna ask me my name?"

"i was just about to."

"No you weren't."

"Yes i was."

"So go ahead."

"i was just trying to think of some super clever way to ask you. It'll probably be the only time i ever will. It's important that i do it right."

"Okay," she says. "Fair enough. I'll wait."

Then, while she waits, she straightens back up and starts to walk the fingers of her right hand up what's left of the ladder pole. See, i knew she was right-handed. Every finger makes a noise like an animal walking. Fingersteps. Four fingertips, one after the other, poke their tops over the ladder-hole opening and start looking around like a curious little pack of animals.

No: one huge heavy-footed spider. It seems to scan the near distance and then it notices me. <u>Really</u> notices me. Slowly, but with a tiny thump on every footfall, it starts to walk across the boards toward my defenseless head. Stopping once or twice to scratch the old wood like it's cleaning a claw.

Thump. Stalk. Thump. Stalk. Scratch. The cabin is so quiet; sounds from outside are totally muffled by the thick hemlock logs, the foam insulation between them. The windows are all closed. Every sound inside the cabin is especially loud: my heartbeat, her breathing near me, the finger thumps. All loud.

Her hand keeps walking. Each finger looks like it is scanning, sniffing, and listening all at the same time. The little beast comes to a stop momentarily when it bumps up against my chin where it is lying on the floor.

God please turn around, i think.

And then it starts to climb my face. i absolutely feel like her hand is some incredibly dangerous animal whose bite could be fatal, but everything will be fine if i just lie totally still, don't even breathe, don't say a word. Just let it do whatever it wants and hope it goes and crawls back in its hole. i'm getting waves of chills hurtling up and down. It's all i can do not to move a muscle. Now it's slowly climbing my chin. It slips back down, gets a toehold on my lips, one paw, i mean one finger, slipping for a second between my lips and grazing my front tooth. It makes it to the cheek--my head is still lying on its side, left cheek on the boards, right one up--it stops, deciding whether to turn left toward my neck or right toward my ear and my hair. It turns right. No, left. No, right. i don't move a muscle. It's moving so lightly now. With every step it tickles my skin.

The outside of my ear. Hesitates where my ear meets my hair. Then with a huge pounce and a growl it grabs the top of my head and shakes it like a hawk seizing a chicken. i scream:

"What's your name?"

She pulls her hand and arm back to the ladder. Crabwalks calmly back down the hole. "Rose Anna. Can I come all the way up?"

"Yeah. Sure," i say, after i get enough breath back to work my voice.

i could stand up while she is bringing the rest of herself onto the loft but i read once that back in the royal courts the highest-status person, the king or queen, got to sit down and everyone else had to stand. i must be really high status if i can just lie here with my hands behind my head, act totally relaxed, maybe fold up my knees a little and cross one leg over the other. i figure it couldn't hurt my cause any to just stay where i am. So i lie there and look up at her looking down at me.

Then i realize that if someone came in and saw us, it would look as if she had just floored me with some martial arts move and is standing there legs apart in victory. Not even breathing hard.

Victor-y.

She offers me her hand. She leans way back and down and pulls and then we're standing very close to each other, facing. Since she has my hand, we turn it into a greeting, and then both drop it at the same instant, embarrassed.

"Happy May Day," she says.

"Is it May Day?"

"Yes," she says, then, "You look nice with your clothes on."

"Thanks. So do you," i say. Before thinking.

Then, i replay those four words in my head to see whether they revealed the relief i feel. That she has clothes on.

See, to my way of thinking, it would be infinitely worse if she realized, from those four words, that i <u>had</u> been lying there seriously picturing the possibility that she was down there naked. i mean, not picturing the possibility. That's not what you picture.

i know that sounds complicated. But when you think a lot, like i do, sometimes you forget that other people are not right alongside of you when you're taking all your own logical leaps. You say something to someone from your point of view, and they're like, how did the conversation get all the way over there? That's when you realize you've been wandering on your own.

"This is my favorite part of the cabin," Rose Anna is saying, ignoring my mental state. Confirming, also, what i thought before: that the cabin was hers just like it was mine. "I like to sit on the corner of the bed and look out the window down the stream. It's the best view."

Let's not go there, i think. Please. After what we've just been through.

"Or," she continues, "I like to lie near where you were lying and look down over the side. The log has chin rest places on it."

"Let's do that," i say.

Then we're lying side by side, nearly touching, with our chins over the log, looking down at the table, the chair, our backpacks, the ROYAL, the pile of paper. There's an old-fashioned-looking pen lying by the paper. From up here it looks like solid gold.

i realize i've been totally in my own mind, thinking about every action of hers in relation to me, to what i was doing.

Maybe she just came up here to write. Like me. Maybe she's been doing that for months. For years. And i never noticed. Now suddenly i'm in <u>her</u> space.

i can see her dog lying right outside the screen door. Some kind of a border collie mix. She's looking through the screen, making good eye contact with us up on the loft.

"What's her name?" i ask.

"Dash. She's a he."

"Does he bite?"

"Oh god yes. If anyone ever threatened me or anything, he'd chew them up. There wouldn't be anything left."

i nod.

Actually i don't really nod, because my chin, like i said, is resting on the peeled log. When a twenty-foot-long, ten-inch-thick hemlock beam is right under your jaw, you don't nod.

10

Rose Anna rolls a little bit onto her side, and i do the same. Now we're lying on our sides facing each other, temples on the beam.

It feels good to think of her with a name.

"Just kidding," she says.

"About what?"

"About Dash. He wouldn't hurt anyone. Well, maybe he would if someone was mugging me or, you know--"

"Yeah."

"But he's a great watchdog. You see his ears?"

He has big stand-up ears like a fox or a bat.

"He hears everything. He lets me know when anyone's coming. Even when they're really far away."

i like that. i'm not very good at seeing or hearing what's coming. Sometimes i think i could use some outside help.

"i like his name," i tell her. "It sounds fast."

"Yeah. Even when he was a puppy he was really fast. We have a place in our house where you can run around the stairs in a circle. You know, out the kitchen, past the front door, stair bottom, living room, other door, kitchen, door, stairs again. Can you picture it?"

"Yes." i think i can, anyway.

"You need to picture a kitchen with two entrances," she says.

"Yeah, i did."

She looks pleased that i can make a mental picture from her words. "He'd run around that circle for hours. I would chase him to get him started, but then once he was wound up he would keep on going."

"Dash," i say.

"Yeah but actually, he was named for Dashiell Hammett."

"Who's that?" i say.

"A writer."

"Oh." Suddenly i want to say, Like me, like you. But i keep it in. Something tells me i should start a list of things we don't need to say. That can be the first thing on the list.

"Of detective stories."

"Wow."

"Black-and-white ones."

i pretend i actually understand what she means by that and don't ask. Then, pretending seems to work, and i do.

"We've been studying Lillian Hellman," she says. "The play-wright."

"You and your mom?"

"Yeah. How did you know?"

"i'm a detective too. Figured you homeschooled. Then i took a logical leap."

She smiles. "I like those."

"Lillian Hellman?" i ask.

"Oh, she wrote plays that used to be famous. Like the one about these two teachers in a girls' school that some bratty students accuse of being lesbians."

"Uh-huh."

"She lived with Dashiell Hammett. She called him Dash. I don't think they ever got married. They drank, and smoked a lot, and made love, but mostly they wrote their books, in two separate rooms. There's a movie about them. They'd show their stuff to each other. When she had just written a page that got her so excited that she couldn't sit down anymore, she would run in and show it to him. Or vice versa. I think he helped her to write skinnier sentences. And she helped him to put more soul in his characters, especially the women."

"Wow."

"You say 'wow' a lot?" she asks.

"When i'm wowed."

She laughs. The sound of her laugh wows me but i just smile. She points her finger toward the dog. "He's my Dash," she says. "If only he could write."

"Like Snoopy," i say.

"Yeah. I'd get him a little portable typewriter and set him up at the table with me and we could do the same thing."

There's an obvious suggestion for me to make at that moment. i mean, she saw what i was doing. But i think, let her make it.

Then she goes somewhere else. "Of course, there's a problem," she says, with this sly look in her eye.

"What's that?"

"If Dash is in here writing with me, he can't be outside doing what he does best, which is keep watch, to warn me with a bark, cause, you know . . ."

"What?"

"You know," she insists, locking her gaze on me.

"i don't think i do," i say, but i do. It's dawning on me. Can this go on the list, i think, of things we don't talk about? But i can tell it's coming. Right now. We're going to talk about it.

"I don't want anyone to see me," she plunges on, "certainly not the way I was yesterday. You know what I mean?"

There are those eyes again.

i must be blushing, like they say, ten shades of crimson--guys can't hide anything--because she laughs. She's mocking me just enough to mean, either, I could mock you a whole lot more here but I've decided not to because I like you and I know you must be feeling disappointed just about now, that you missed the peep show, guys hate to miss stuff like that, or, the whole direction of this conversation is a total fib and if I laughed too hard you would realize that.

It's like this TV comedy i saw once about some sex thing where everyone knew what the subject was but no one ever actually came out and said the word--

i finally find my voice. "You mean you were really--?"

"Guess you missed it," she says.

"Yeah well i wouldn't have <u>seen</u> anything anyway because like you say your dog would have heard me coming, and--"

"And what?" she asks.

"And he would have barked."

"And?" She's not going to let me off easy.

"You would have had time to get your clothes back on."

There, i said it. i'm the first one who said the actual words.

"Right. But would I have?"

She laughs again. She has me. i look right into her eyes, trying to read her expression.

There is the slightest possibility, i have to admit, though i think it's a very small one, that if i had come yesterday, and if she was, you know, totally naked, and if the dog had barked, and if she had looked around and seen me coming across the clearing, that she would have decided, on the spot, to stay just the way she was. A kind of payback. Making things equal between us. Assuming, once i saw her, i would be too embarrassed to come in. Or even to look for more than a second. Which is all the look she got of me.

i mean, i think it was all she got.

That is, if this whole conversation isn't a tease. She's that good an actress, i'll probably never know.

So i change the subject.

"i'm a writer," i say. Although, right away i realize that sounds like bragging. Coming here like i've done for three days to hunt out the story stuck in the ROYAL doesn't really earn me the right to call myself a writer.

"I know," she says. "I got what you were doing."

i let that go by.

"Plus," she goes on, "you brought that typewriter all the way up here. That couldn't have been easy."

"We could write together," i blurt out. "You and me. Show each other stuff."

"Sure," she says. "But don't get any ideas."

"No." That's what you say when you are full of ideas.

"Okay, let's get started," she says. "Actually I already did. Yesterday. A story. Well, kind of a story."

She's already up and pulling on my arm. Like she has all these ideas and she's anxious to climb down there and get to it. With her gold fountain pen.

So now we're standing, facing each other. Her head comes up just a few inches below mine. i'm still in my growth spurt, she must be done with hers, she looks more grown up than me, especially around her eyes, well, her hips, too. Girls--

"Don't look at me that way," she says, reading my thought.

"Sorry." Man, she doesn't miss anything.

"I'm sixteen," she says, "since you asked." Which i hadn't. And then she adds, "Aquarius." So now i'll know what month she was born in, once i go home and look it up.

i guess i keep staring at her too hard, i have to work on that, because when you can't think of what to say next, and you're running over the possibilities in your mind, your eyes can go blank and it's hard not to look like you're using X-ray vision on the person you're talking to.

"Built for speed, not for comfort," she says, and right away she's back down the ladder. i know i would never be able to catch her--in a race up the trail, or zigzagging through trees, or running anywhere--unless she wanted me to.

i follow her down at my own pace and face her again at the bottom.

"So are we going to start?" she asks. Waving the gold pen.

"i can't," i say. "i mean i can't today. i really have to go. We're going on a family trip. i'm almost late, i have to get back."

Her face shows this flash of disappointment, but then that changes to a smile. "To number 26 Highlawn?"

"Yes!" i say. She has me again. By the name tag.

She looks at me. "Okay. Fair enough. So when <u>can</u> we start?"

"How about Tuesday?" Whoa, am i, are we, actually making a date here? What kind of a date? i've never done that before.

"Okay."

"After school?" i say.

"After <u>your</u> school."

She moves to the chair on the far side of the table from where i have the ROYAL set up. She opens the deck window like she's done it a hundred times and sits down, her back to it. She starts acting like she's getting ready, physically and mentally, for her day's work. i don't move yet. She shuffles some papers and then looks up at me like i've come looking for a job and she's surprised i'm still there, the interview being over a long time ago.

"See you then. I'll be watching for you," she says. "We can come up together."

"Watching where?"

"From my house. I'll be waiting on the porch. I'll have this same stuff on, so you'll recognize me."

"i won't need anything—" i start to say, and then i realize she's joking. Keep up with her, man. "Which house is yours?"

"The yellow one, with the green shutters. Needs paint. Just up from the Free Farm."

"The Free Farm?" i ask.

"The Franklin farm. My mom lived on a commune out near Green River—"

"Hey, my mom did, too. i mean, probably not the same one, but on a commune—"

"Cool. Anyway, Mr. Franklin used to take them a lot of stuff

for free. Eggs and milk and blankets and stuff. Firewood. Old
tools. They used to come over to his place to take showers,
and use the phone. He never wanted any money for anything
so they called it the Free Farm."

"Wow."

"My mom talks about it all the time cause she ended up living right across the road from it, and now it's empty. She goes
to visit him sometimes at the Lodge."

i like the name Free Farm better than "the old Franklin
place." i bet Franklin liked it better, too. Free Farm. i'll bet he
never got married cause he was too shy, not free at all, and he
liked to ride out to their commune, help out, flirt a little, a lot
actually, look at the women going topless, and when he got
back home he drank instant coffee and ate Wonder bread,
and looked at himself in his one ratty bathroom mirror, and
wished he didn't live in such a run-down lonely place. Helping
a bunch of young people get through winter was the best thing
he did. Maybe ever did. i'll bet he still thinks of it all the time.

This picture of an old guy i never even saw or thought of, in
a nursing home with all his memories, jumps into my head just
like that with the details all filled out, i swear, and it makes me
wonder what the heck is going on with my mind. Is it the
ROYAL, or is it because Rose Anna is here with me? Is it
both?

i wish i could stay. Sit and be with her and write stuff like
that last bit down. Show it to her. Be like Lillian and Dash, do
it all. All except for the smoking and drinking. But instead i
make myself reach down and swing the backpack with my
name on it over my shoulder.

"Well. Goodbye," she says.

"Goodbye." Then i just stand there. "You sure you don't want to walk out together?"

"No, I'm staying, remember?" she says. "Got some writing to do. Right now. I'm working on this idea."

"You are?" i guess i'm stalling.

"Yeah. I told you. Look." She shows me a half-done drawing and some words.

"Is that a lizard?" i ask.

"No. It's a red-spotted newt. The kind of salamander you find around here."

"What's he doing?"

"She. And I don't really want to tell you. It's bad luck."

i look for a while more, even though i don't have time to spare.

"It's going to be about global warming," she says. "It's about this meeting that some animal spirits have, to discuss putting out a big sign, to warn the human race before it's too late."

She points down to the newt. "She's going to the meeting. It's an ecofeminist fable. That's what I like to write. That and my tracking journal."

"Tracking journal?"

"That's where I get my ideas from. But no more now. You have to go!"

"All right." i don't like her telling me i have to leave her, but she's right. "Lock up when you leave."

"Of course." She knows what i meant by lock up.

"It's my uncle's cabin."

"Oh." Her expression says that means nothing at all to her. i mean, that somebody owns the place. Or that anybody anywhere owns anything.

"It's a great place to write, isn't it?" i say, looking around.

"Well, yeah."

"i wish i could stay," i tell her. i could have left that unsaid, but sometimes it's important to put stuff out there even when you know it's already understood.

"I know," she says, "but--" She's almost pushing me out. Just with her words i mean.

i take a few steps toward the door. Hear some paws on the porch. "See you Tuesday," i say. Trying to make it sound casual.

"Nice to meet you," she says. But in a different voice, like a mother or a teacher who's reminding you of your manners.

"Oh, yeah. Sorry. Me, too. i mean, you, too."

It feels strange to leave her there like that, in my cabin. Okay, her cabin, too.

"Say hi to Dash when you walk by him. Let him sniff your hand."

"Okay."

He smells, wags, and stretches. Got it.

"Goodbye," i call back in to her, even though i've already said it. i close the door gently so it won't slam. "Have a good time writing!"

She hollers out to me, "I will."

i take a few more slow steps along the deck, and then the stairs and the ground. She calls out to me again.

"Victor!"

i stop. "What?"

"Don't look back!"

11

May 4

Tuesday couldn't come quick enough for me. Then, the school day drags even more than usual.

At 2:30 i hurtle away from the bike rack. Then right away i get stuck. Fifteen school buses are turning at the light. Moving so slow! When they're gone, there's smoke and diesel soot everywhere.

When i get out to Bonnyvale i don't see her, not up on her porch or coming down the road. She's not going to keep the date. i'll never see her again.

Then, i look across Franklin's pasture. She's sitting on the stone wall, right where the woods trail starts.

i think she chose that spot so we can watch each other while i cross the field. i'm right back where i was on Saturday, not knowing what to say, or when to say it. i mean, do you shake hands, or start a conversation, or just start walking together? Do you act casual, like, Hey, we do this all the time, or do you let her know how special it feels?

So i crouch down and pet her dog.

i look up and there she is right next to me, smiling down,

like she's welcoming me to her woods. Her hair is even wilder than before, and she's in those two red T-shirts again, everything sparkling--beads, earrings, sunlight, eyes, teeth, little hairs on her arms. She stretches, which lifts her shirts up from her jeans, and there's her stomach all bright and sunlit.

She breaks the ice. "How was school?"

"It was okay. This is going to be better." That just comes out without thinking.

"I know," she says, almost sympathetically. She's been out all day exploring while i was shut in.

We set off walking, through the gap in the stone wall, and the right turn uphill. i stash the bike. Dash hangs behind her. That puts me third. Which is okay by me. i won't have to keep up conversation, i can just watch her. She must feel me watching her too hard, cause she stops and waits for me to fall in beside her.

"We have to walk really close together," she says. i don't know what she means--is that what she wants, to be close to me? Or is this some sort of game and that's rule number one? She must realize i don't get it.

She points. The footpath leads uphill--there's branches leaning in, and pools of sunlight. "I mean," she says, "it's a narrow trail. So if we walk side by side we have to be careful. There are so many things just beginning to grow, we don't want to step on them. If we walk too wide we can ruin all their plans."

i didn't know that flowers have plans. Or mosses or ferns, or wild strawberry plants. Do they all have plans?

Side by side now. i'm feeling and hearing every place where we brush against each other. Not really aware of anything else.

Then suddenly she kneels down and shows me a little pink flower i'd come close to crushing. i bend down too, and i see that there are dozens of them, all stripy pink and white, each with a bright dot of yellow in the middle. i would have walked right over them and left them for dead.

For the first time we're both actually still, not moving or speaking. i'm inches away from her face. i would stay right here, not wanting to move, waiting to see more and more in her eyes, but she pulls me up and back into gear in one quick motion.

We're walking again. Then, while riffling through potential conversation topics, i think of one thing that might work, something that's still stuck in my mind.

"Tracking journal?"

"I track animals," she says right away, like it's okay with her to pick up a conversation where it stopped, even after a three-day gap. "I read sign. You're supposed to keep a journal of everything you notice. Do an entry, or a sketch. Then if you have to look stuff up later you have your description. You can add more to it. Or use it for ideas." She stops walking and shows me a little red cloth notebook tied up with a button and string. Pulls it out of her back pocket.

"Neat," i say. "Will you show me?"

"No, it's like my diary. It's not for consumption." She has this strange, almost wild animal look in her eyes. Like a raccoon or something that you see in the woods. You think for a second it's going to run right at you and then of course it runs in the opposite direction.

"No," i say. "Not the journal. i mean show me stuff you see. Out here."

"Well I will if you'll be quiet and let me concentrate."

"Okay."

"Okay then."

"But--" There's one more thing.

She stops and breathes out, a breath you can hear, pretending to be annoyed. "What?"

"What was that look about, just then?" See, i need to show her that i can notice stuff, too. Maybe not footprints, but i'm pretty good at tracks that thoughts leave on a face.

She has to think for a minute, whether to tell me or not. Then she does. "You're in it."

"In what?"

"In my tracking journal. You're an entry."

Oh, great. She <u>was</u> stalking me.

Then she pushes the journal with me in it back deep in her pocket, with a little flicker of I-dare-you-to-reach-in-there-and-try-to-pull-it-out. She pats it and turns and heads up toward the steep part of the trail. Where i almost threw the ROYAL over.

i don't try to catch up with her. But if she's feeling anything like me, she must realize that side by side almost touching is not going to work. Not if we're ever going to notice anything else.

Walking behind her doesn't work too well for me, either. i get distracted watching her. And i want to know what she's written about me.

For a second i think about stopping and sneaking back downhill. Just to imagine the expression on her face when she turns around and sees i'm not there.

Dash looks back to see if i'm keeping up. Dogs will do that, if they're walking with two people. i can read <u>his</u> expression all right. It says, Stick with us, just give her some space, keep quiet and she'll start showing us what she finds.

And she does. She shows us a lot. A red squirrel nest high up in a maple. Two sets of deer prints in the wet spot. Deer go single file, too.

"Look at this," she says, farther up the trail.

There's an old grapevine about as thick as my arm, wound around a yellow birch. They almost seem to be holding each other up, getting thinner near their tops, maybe sixty feet over our heads, but still wound together. i guess if the vine ever had any grapes, they would be for birds only.

"They grew up together," she says.

We both lean back, trying to see up through all the leaves and branches. We bump into each other, and i'm this close to reaching for her hand, but i don't.

Farther along, she shows me an orangey mushroom she says used to be famous for giving people visions. There's one bite taken out of it. Some animal. Porcupine maybe, or skunk--she can't quite tell from the mouth shape. There's no sign that he spit the mouthful out.

"Whoever it was," she says, "knew just how much to eat. No more and no less. Take too much and you die."

i get this image in my head of a possum or woodchuck lying nearby stretched out on his back seeing heaven. Eyes wide. Smiling. Pink tongue hanging out to the side. Front paws folded on his belly, little furry chest pumping up and down. i tell her and she laughs.

We come to a patch in the sugarbush where the old leaves look really deep and dry. Rose Anna sits down all of a sudden and stretches out her legs and starts throwing the leaves all around herself.

At first i think she's playing, but then she looks up at me with her eyes wide. She has this look on her face i've never seen before on anyone--like she's vibrating from deep inside.

"I'm so scared. Scared of what this year's leaves are going to be like."

i have no idea what she's talking about.

"Last year so many of them were small. They never grew big, and during foliage season a lot of them got black spots and then turned gray and fell off early. It was the worst autumn ever."

She holds up a leaf. "See, it doesn't look right. There's no color."

i remember. The newspapers said that October in Vermont was the warmest in history, the leaves hadn't turned all bright and colorful like they do. They needed frost, and there wasn't any. Tourist numbers were way down, too. i saw this cartoon of someone spraying red and yellow paint from an airplane so the foliage would look like it was supposed to.

"Can you imagine what it would be like around here if the sugar maples were gone, or maybe we still had them, but they were all sick and didn't make any syrup? And there was no deep snow here anymore, ever?"

i think about it now, about the planet heating up. Vermont without maple trees or deep snow. One of my favorite things is seeing all the sugarhouses chugging away in March. Big plumes of smoke. i mean steam. i don't eat much of the stuff, cause i have a salty tooth, my mom says, but still, i would miss it. But that's not the point. Everyone knows that if Vermont warms up so much that the maples get sick, it means other places will be flooding and drowning. Or turning into deserts. It makes me look at all the budding leaves around us in a whole new way. And i'm worried now, too. This year, it was the worst maple syrup season ever. All the farmers said the sap didn't run right.

She gets up and we walk on, underneath all those maple leaves just starting out new and pale green. We come to the knoll just above the cabin. The trail turns to the left, and suddenly there it is: the clearing, with the cabin--every one of its logs different--and the window she saw me through. No matter what the time of day, the cabin glows, like it's calling you, like something amazing is waiting for you inside.

"i always stop here for a few seconds and look at it," i say. "And listen."

"So do I."

"You do?"

She nods. "I heard you typing."

12

We pull open the heavy wooden door, and the screen, and go in together.

My ROYAL is sitting there like an old Model T Ford, waiting for me to crank it so we can go for a ride.

Rose Anna stands beside the table and looks up at the loft where i was hiding three days ago, heart pounding, afraid of what she was doing down here. She looks back at me and starts to giggle, remembering.

"What?" i say.

"Are you decent?" she asks, in a perfect imitation of my froggy voice.

i'm never going to live that one down.

Then, she touches the ROYAL. Runs her hands over the keys, making the letter levers flip up and down, and pushes a silver tab on the end that slides the carriage over till the bell goes off.

"It's beautiful," she says.

We sit down and get to work. Backpacks off. Paper out.

Real professional, on opposite sides of the table. Me in my usual seat and Rose Anna with her back to the deck window. Both with jobs to do.

Actually not yet, because before we start, she shows me what she worked on when i couldn't stay on Saturday. And i take my stack out of my backpack.

i'm thinking, i was the one who asked for this. To show each other. But suddenly i think, Whoa, do i really want to? Did she show me her tracking journal? Who is she, anyway? Did you see that look in her eyes? Can i trust her? Then i hear the words in my head again--saying "Do it," and i watch myself push the papers across the table toward her.

We make a deal--that we won't comment. Just look, read. Take it in. Not say a word. That seems important to both of us, though i'm not sure why.

The Summit Meeting

There's not a mammal that lives in my woods that I haven't tracked. But there are animals that don't leave tracks or sign. Salamanders are too light-footed. You see them by surprise when you're following something else.

Twice, I've seen an ordinary red-spotted newt—Notoph-thalmus viridescens—in a very unusual place.

There is a little stream way up in the woods. I was trying to look through the sunlight on the surface of a pool, to see whether brook trout came so far upstream, and right in the middle of the waterfall below the pool, there it was: a bright red-orange newt bouncing up and down on a broken-off piece of hazel root.

"Newts, huh?" i say.

She looks up at me with a withering, interrupted look. "Yeah."

"So, uh, what is it about newts? And why 'summit meeting'? Isn't that like when world leaders get together?"

She puts my papers back down on the table. "Are you going to read and not comment like we said, or is the deal off already?"

"Right," i say. "i forgot."

"So, can you just wait and see?"

"Sure. No problem." i pick up where i left off:

. . . a bouncing bright red-orange newt bouncing up and down on a broken-off piece of hazel root. She had to grip the root really hard, to not fall off. Her little amphibian brain was being pounded by water, while her body jiggled up and down. If a newt could look like she was having a good time, she did.

i look over at Rose Anna. She's still frowning at me, not back reading yet. What a face.

"Sorry," i say, drawing the word out.

She just snorts. But she looks back down at my story, and i see a little smile run past her lips.

i read more of hers:

I was afraid she would fall off. So, gently, I picked her up and put her on solid ground. Even though you're really not supposed to interfere.

I said, "You don't want to be swept away!"

She looked up at me.

And that's when the idea for the story came to me:

In the pool above the fall, the sunlight suddenly goes dark. Raindrops hit the water, then ripples move out from them, and then more drops. A drizzle first, then a downpour! The pool fills up with twigs and leaves and grasses and things—washed down from above—but it all gets stuck between two rocks, plugged up just above where Oona Newt is dancing!

"Oona Newt?" i ask.

"Shut up. Just shut up."

"Okay."

All of a sudden the plug gives way and everything rushes over the brink, comes down on her, breaks her hazel root, and she screams—if newts can scream—as she slams into the water. She comes up gasping, shooting off downstream, clutching a piece of the root, which has now become her life raft.

Oh no, she thinks, oh no I'm going to die! oh no hold on just hold on!

That's all there is. i send it back across the table. There's lots i could say about it, i mean i have a reaction, but we've agreed not to, at least not yet. That's the deal. After a while she realizes that i'm done, and she's nowhere near finished mine.

"You have a lot more than me," Rose Anna says.

"i know." Then all of a sudden i hear myself saying, "Do you want to take it home?"

Instantly i think, Whoa, where did that come from? What ever happened to thinking about something before you say it?

You think you're holding on in the usual way, maybe dancing a little bit for fun, and then you get swept away--

"Yes," she says, before i can take it back. "Is that okay?"

i'm not sure. There's so much in there that's personal, that nobody knows about me. i mean i already decided she could read it, but letting it out of my sight, letting her take it home, that feels different.

Then i picture her in her room with the door shut, in whatever kind of chair she has, no, wait, it's a lot later and she's lying on her bed--in her bed--with her knees up, reading my words piled on her lap. It's like i'm with her.

The whole house is dark, the rest of her family's asleep, and she has this little bed light on. She doesn't have a real bedtime or get-up time, cause she's homeschooled. She's twirling one of the kinks in her hair. She's reading all that stuff about how we met, about me, the yard sale, and Will's room, everything. Maybe she's still wearing the two red T-shirts, or no, maybe she-- Whoa!

i yank my mind back to the cabin. She gives me a big smile. Waves to me, like she can see where I've been, and she's amazed i can travel so far in just a second or two and land right back in the same place.

"Is it okay?" she repeats.

"i guess so."

"You guess so? You offered and you guess so?"

"i mean yes, it's okay. It's fine," i say.

"I'll give it back to you next time," she says.

So, there's going to be a next time.

Then we write separately but together, which is what we really made the date to do. See if we can. i mean, with the other person right there.

It's an adjustment. i mean, it certainly isn't what i planned when i lugged the ROYAL out here. But like i said, i'm learning to go along with things i don't completely understand. At least i don't have to think about what to write about.

Sounds come in from outside, and we make sounds, too. Time goes by, i guess, cause when i finally look up, the light has changed. We need to leave soon. i don't want to stay past the time when i'd have to tell my parents why i'm late getting home. What would i say?

Plus, we need time to read.

There's a moment when the ROYAL rings its last bell and the tip of Rose Anna's pen stops moving, scratching across the paper. Suddenly it gets quiet. Then we push our work across the table toward each other.

Oona Newt was different from the others in her pack. She liked to go off by herself, to find out what was out there, what was beyond the known edges of their clearing. Sometimes she would even go to a pond nearby, to sit on the shore and watch the older newts swimming under the water, wishing she could communicate with them, but they don't see what's out there on land, they have no memory of what they were before.

The other newts warned her that sometime she'd pay the price for being so different from the rest, for going off by herself all the time. Now, as she's swept away in the flood, she thinks, How right they were!

*If I can just keep my head above water, she thinks, and hang
on! Now the stream breaks out of its banks and becomes a flood.
She whizzes by this huge ash tree—she'd seen it only once before;
it was the border of her world. It's standing in the floodwater
now—if only she could let go and grab it and somehow still make
it home, bruised and soaked but at least alive, but she's past it in
a second—*

*It's flooded everywhere. Oona is one bright red moving dot
among all the muddy browns and grays, and other animals—
frogs, turtles, ducklings, muskrats—all of them in trouble.*

*Oona is so waterlogged, she's barely alive. Somehow she hasn't
sunk yet. She can't see, can't even hear, the danger ahead. But just
a few yards away, the whole flood is pouring over a broken
beaver dam!*

*All the animals caught in the flood try desperately to swim
back the other way, but it's impossible. They flail at the water,
then shriek as they go over the edge. Then, just as Oona hears the
screams and the huge crush of falling water and pond junk, and
she's about to go over to her death, she hears—*

"Let go!!!"

—and she does just what the voice says, she

"Hey," i say, "i didn't know that!"

"Didn't know what?" Rose Anna is spitting the words out
slow, to show how bothered she is.

"That newts can talk to each other, like people do."

"Read."

"Let go!!!"

—and she does just what the voice says, she lets go of the root

she's been gripping all this while, and, suddenly lighter, it shoots up up up and over the falls, disappears. In the instant that Oona sees this, she sinks and slams her chest against a log. She folds and twists, it's all pounding water and bubbles and foaming pond scum and no way to tell what's up and what's down, and then the tip of her tail breaks above water, and a little four-fingered hand grabs it and yanks her out.

i look up. Carried away for a minute, like Oona in the flood, but i'm still right here. Rose Anna is, too.

There's this new feeling in the cabin. It's as if some energy that has been waiting here all these years, something stuck between the logs, started to come out when i came here with the ROYAL, and then more when i was writing naked--but now that Rose Anna and i are both here, it's really out, and it's not going to go back into hiding.

It stays with us after we close up, while we walk back down and out to the road. We make a plan to meet again. We pause, not really knowing how to do a goodbye. She starts uphill to her house, and i coast down on my bike. We don't touch hands or anything, but i can still feel it. It doesn't go away.

i wonder if she feels it, too.

Whatever it is, it's affected my vision. Everything looks different. It's hard to explain. i need a metaphor.

It's like a lens. Like i'm wearing this new pair of glasses all the time now, that i'm looking through, out at the world. Or, more like a bubble, because it's not just in front of me, it's in a circle around my head. But it's not one of those bubbles that pops. It stays. It's thick. Like an old deep-sea diver's glass helmet--

13

i'm here watching Rose Anna as she writes and draws. She works slow. She thinks a lot before moving the pen. Sometimes she sucks on it and gets black on her lips. i wish i could--

Oh man.

i stop writing. Show me your next part, i think. Or did i actually say it? She stops. We look at each other and both laugh, as if something had just tickled us at the same time. A telepathic thought, maybe. Like we're inside the same bubble, looking out.

i watch Rose Anna concentrate when she writes, or draws, and when she reads my writing. She really reads. My old ROYAL, when i type hard, the type almost cuts through the paper, it's three-dimensional. i've watched her almost try to read it with her fingertips.

She feels and sees stuff i don't even notice. That must be what being a tracker means. Plus, she sees in both directions, way little and way big. And from angles i didn't even know existed. Like what things might look like from a newt's eye, or from out of a crack in a rock.

She sees implications, too. She'll hold a maple leaf up to the light to look at the detail, and right away it's more than a leaf, it's a lung, or a river delta, it's the whole planet, the climate changing, the North Pole melting, Vermont losing its syrup-- all that in one leaf with one small black spot on it. And then, she gets that look like something is about to erupt inside her, so get out of the way, and meanwhile here i am sitting across the table writing about mountain bikes, old typewriters, yard sales, log cabins, and slowpoke school buses.

Oona is on a tiny piece of solid ground. She looks down:

Tons of water pummeling rocks, and big sticks and logs smashing to bits on the bottom. And right in the middle, like a wormhole, a whirlpool, all the water and pond junk are spinning faster than seems possible and vanishing into this bottomless black pit of death.

She turns away from it and sees who rescued her. Another newt, a little bigger, a browner shade of red.

"My name's Amoss. Are you okay?"

She's soaking wet, and bruised, but says, "I think so. I'm Oona. Thank you for saving me."

Amoss: "Had no choice. Saw you from far away. You're lucky you're so easy to see. You were comin' right at me."

"Newts talking again. Amazing," i say.

"Personification," Rose Anna says. "You do it, too. You said so."

"Right."

"*Funny, I was just sitting here thinking I needed company on my trip today. I guess you're it.*"

"*What kind of trip?*" Oona asks.

"*You see that hilltop up there? Above the trees? The one with the bare rock top?*"

"*I see it,*" she says.

"*That's called Owl's Head Mountain. That's where we're going.*"

The rain has stopped now, and shafts of sunlight pierce the clouds. One really bright sun ray hits the edge of Owl's Head and sparkles for a moment, a star-shaped sparkle, like there might be something magical up there.

Oona asks, "Do you know the way?"

"*Oh, I don't have to. We're meeting my teacher at the end of the dam. He knows the way.*"

Oona just nods. She's tired, soaked, and aching, but game for the journey. Amoss gives her his hand to start her going.

14

"Is it the pen?" i ask her. We're back in the cabin, and Rose Anna is bent over her work. i'm not doing anything. She's been ignoring me, but that's okay, cause that's part of the deal.

"What do you mean?" she says. Like, Where did that question come from all of a sudden?

"i mean, if i wrote with a solid gold fountain pen--"

"It's not solid gold."

"Whatever. Would my writing come out all fictional like yours?"

"You love typing. Don't you?"

"Yes, but it's so mechanical. And noisy."

"I like the noise," she says. "I like the table shaking, too."

"That's my knees."

"No it's not; it's the typewriter."

"i wish i could write like you do. Think the way you do."

She looks right at me. "Well, you can't. You write like you and I write like me. Same with thinking."

i can tell she is playing with me. Today for some reason i

can't write. i feel like a mountain climber stuck on a ledge, feet hurting, pack heavy. Wondering why i started. Can't move up or down. She's trying to get me up and going again.

"Anyway you can't use my pen. I have to."

She holds it up for me to look at.

"My grandmother gave it to me. She just moved into one of those senior places. In New York State. She got rid of almost everything first. I helped her for a whole week last winter, going through stuff. You wouldn't believe the stuff old people save. I kept lugging these huge garbage bags of junk out to the Dumpster."

"Muscles," i say, for no reason. It's like i'm hungry for any new way to think about her for when we're not together, and when i get a new one i add it to the whole picture.

"Yeah. We went through all her drawers and closets," she says. "See when you're homeschooled you can take a week off for something like that and call it history. So it's like you're still in school."

She gets up and comes around to my side of the table. She never did that before. We always have this old oak table full of stories between us. Like we're more comfortable that way, without saying it. She leans really close behind me and puts her left hand on my left shoulder--casually, only--and shows me the pen close up. She's resting her chin on the side of the top of my head.

"See, it's gold-plated."

i'm listening, but it's her leaning on me that i'm thinking about.

"One day my gram was looking through a dresser, and she went 'Ooooh, look what I just found!' and she got all mysterious. She showed me this little red Chinese silk bag and opened it up, real slow, and pulled this pen out."

"Wow."

"That's what I said. 'Wow.' Then she got all sentimental about it, how long she'd had it, how much it meant to her, how valuable it was, and then when she was finished, she gave it to me. Told me to use it well."

Now i feel like we're on familiar ground. Glad to be there.

"She told me this whole story about the pen. She bought it at some store in England. They have these little towns there with funny names like Norton-in-the-Fens and little streets with rows of little shops, you know, greengrocers, butchers, real estate agents, hatters, stationers. That's where she got it, at a stationers. It's a real fountain pen with the little rubber squeezy bag inside. The bladder."

The pen has a brushed checkerboard pattern all over it, gold crisscrossed two ways. It says "SWAN" on the clip, and "Made in England." The tip is gold, too.

"She said it's about seventy years old. Not quite as old as she is."

"Wow."

"Yeah. Feel it. It's really heavy."

i take it and hold it for a second. i can almost feel its age and all the people who held it before. It's the kind of thing where you know right away it's top quality. Like my ROYAL. Although definitely not as hard to lug uphill.

"Did she tell you it had a story stuck in it?" i say, putting it back in her hand.

"In what?"

"In the pen," i say, thinking, This is so obvious. Didn't she read what i wrote?

"No," she says.

i'm disappointed.

After a few seconds she says, "It's in the ink."

"What?"

"The ink. She made her own ink, out of burnt-up deer bones and blackberries and dried possum blood or something. She couldn't remember. She said she mooshed everything up in a mortar and pestle. Which one is the mortar and which is the pestle?"

"i don't know." i never thought about which is which. It's like they mean something as a couple but not on their own.

"She said some white witch taught her the recipe."

"Oooh, scary," i whisper.

i can see her glaring at me out of the corner of my eye. "They did this chanting over it, she says, and mixed it with this special well water, and she had big plans to write some fantasy with her magic ink. My grandma's into Druid stuff. She's a Wiccan. You know, hazel bushes, stone circles, Tarot cards, almanacs, house altars."

i don't know, i'm thinking. Rose Anna knows about all these things i've hardly even heard about.

"You do know about stuff like that, don't you?" She's still in back of me but she leans farther to the side and to the table, so our eyes can meet.

"Sure," i say quickly. But when she's looking right at me from two inches away, i have to tell the truth. "Actually i don't."

"Wiccan," she explains, "means white witchcraft. It's socially acceptable, positive, female. It's the fastest growing religion in America."

"Faster than that born-again Jesus stuff?"

"Well yeah. Because it started smaller. See, when men took over the world, they said, Hey, let's not share power with women anymore. So they crushed the goddess religion, which was everywhere. They said it was all evil, dirty witchcraft and stamped it out. Till almost nothing was left. Really, they wrecked the temples, burned the libraries, killed about ten million innocent women, i mean, after having sex with them first, of course. What else? Oh yeah, they took over all the holidays, too. Gave 'em different names."

"i didn't know about that, either."

"Of course not. They don't advertise what they did. It's taken them about four thousand years. But they never quite finished the job."

"They didn't?"

"No, they never got it all. That's how it can come back now. They missed a few pockets of it. Like little tiny embers left after all the witches got burned. Pieces of bone still on fire."

"Like in The Crucible?" i say. "We read that last year."

"Exactly. Oh man, those creepy guys in their long coats? Spying on the campfire dances? To gather evidence, right-- they got all excited, so then they started hating themselves for getting excited, and had to hang us. Or burn us or drown us. It was either that or--I don't know what."

"You were there?" i look up at her with pretend wide eyes. "i don't remember seeing you."

She likes that one. Picturing me at midnight with a long

beard and an itchy wool jacket, watching her from behind an oak tree. Her naked skin in the firelight burning my eyes.

i go back to where we were.

"So, are you a Wiccan, too? Like your grandma?"

"I think so," she says. "It's not like there's any paper you have to sign. You just kind of flow into it."

She laughs like "flow" is some kind of inside joke.

i show off my anthropological knowledge. "Yeah, but have you been initiated?"

"Of course."

"Tell me about it."

"No way."

After absorbing that blow, i ask, "Did she ever write it?"

"Did who ever write what?"

"Your grandma. Her story."

"I don't think so," she says. "The ink bottle was still full when she gave it to me. She said, 'I probably won't use this now, dear, I'm too old. You write something with it.' "

Sounds like a theme here, i think. The yard sale guy and now her granny. How do you get too old to write? i wonder. What happens? Can't see the keys anymore? Your ink goes dry? Or you do? You squeeze your writing bladder and nothing comes out.

Rose Anna's still leaning over me. She puts the pen back in my hand and i make some squiggles on a piece of paper. Smooth--the pen's almost leading my hand over the page. It's so different from tapping on typewriter keys, my arm starts dancing right away. In just a few seconds my one ink line branches off into little twigs and leaves, like it's alive. Keep this up and i'll be drawing lizards, too.

"See, you're an artist," she says.

She stops leaning on me. It feels to me like she has to pull herself away, like she doesn't really want to leave. She takes the pen and goes back to her seat, smiles at me, bends over her writing again. i can still feel every place where she was touching me. i sit there wondering if she can feel it, too. Where her chin was against my temple. Her handprint on my shoulder. Tingles in my back.

Victor. Get a grip.

i'm quiet for a while. i'm thinking, i should run back to town after this, go up Greenleaf, and thank the guy for sticking me with that typewriter. Thank him or blame him. i make a mental note to go see him again.

But what would i tell him? Hey mister because of you i met this young witch, i mean, she found _me_. i was naked. i'm an entry in her tracking journal. i think i'd like to join her group, her tribe, whatever they call it--

"So, is it only women?" i ask, interrupting her at her work.

She puts the pen down and looks back with fake exasperation. She's probably also wondering where my mind has gotten to now. It's like a dog that'll go anywhere if you don't keep it tied up.

"Only women?" she says.

"In your religion."

"I didn't say it _was_ my religion. I said I _thought_ it was. Anyway, it's not really a religion in the ordinary sense. There are no leaders, and how you practice it is totally up to you."

i still want to know. "But are there only women in it?"

"No. We're looking for a few good men."

"Oh, like the Marines."

"Exactly. Different kind of men, though."

"So," i continue, still really enjoying the conversation, and looking for a compliment, "what kind of men would you be looking for? i mean, maybe i qualify."

"Guys who don't mind Really Strong Women." She pauses for a second, then she asks, "Do you mind them? I mean us?"

"No, of course not."

"Have you ever slept with a Really Strong Woman?" she asks me. See, why is it that even when we're just sitting still i feel like Rose Anna's racing ahead of me and i'm trying to catch up? She's like, Catch me quick before I turn into something you don't recognize.

"Always," i say, "they're the most fun. In bed, anyway."

Got there ahead of her for once. i'm learning. She balls up a blank piece of paper and throws it at me across the table, but she misses.

Then we just sit like we usually do, across the table, both working. Except this time we're both smiling down at our work.

And again, before we leave, we read.

Amoss and Oona pick their way toward the end of the dam. It's still dangerous, with waterfalls to cross, and big floating branches that could knock them over the brink if they didn't jump out of the way. Once or twice they have to ferry on an improvised boat—a piece of curled birch bark or a beaver-chewed poplar stick.

Oona tries to speak over the roar of the water. "What's the trip about?"

"*There's a meeting," Amoss shouts. "A summit meeting. It's really important.*"

"*A what?*"

"*A SUMMIT MEETING!*"

"*Oh.*"

A little later she asks, "Who's your teacher?"

"*His name is Solemn Andrew.*"

"*Who?*"

"*SOLEMN ANDREW!*"

Finally they make it to an old silver birch stump with ferns growing out of the top and reindeer lichen, and moss along its north side. Right next to it, Solemn Andrew is waiting.

He is the biggest, oldest, saddest-looking salamander Oona has ever seen. He kind of glistens: shiny slate gray with dull yellowish speckles all over him. With eyes full of love and patience, and a reassuring, but raspy, voice:

"*You made it, Amoss.*"

"*No problem," Amoss says, even though it was a hard trip.*

"*And you've got company," Solemn Andrew says.*

Amoss introduces Oona, who announces, "He saved my life."

Amoss looks proud. Newt-proud.

Solemn Andrew takes a few slow steps toward her and looks into her face. Oona looks back at him unblinking. She feels like he can see into her past and future, see all the land and water stages of her life cycle with no effort at all. Even see her splashing in the waterfall, then nearly drowning—

"*Come in on the flood, did you?" he asks her.*

She turns even redder and nods.

He starts lumbering away. Oona and Amoss fall in behind. Solemn Andrew has a funny walk, like the kind you develop when you get old and you have to make adjustments to joints and things that don't work so well anymore. It's part slither, part limp, part crazy puppet dance—

They don't look up as they walk, but if they did, they would see Owl's Head Mountain looming above the trees. It looks closer already. Then it starts to sink behind the treetops. That's how you can tell that they're getting near to the woods.

15

May 14

i told my mother about Rose Anna.

No particular reason i chose my mom and not my dad. You only have to tell one of them anything. The other one will find out soon enough.

We were in the car, just her and me, on the way back from my annual "physical," where Dr. Shaeffer pokes me a lot and looks at me seriously, then cracks a few jokes and tells me stuff about myself i already know.

The silence in the car seemed uncomfortable. Probably because i felt like i was hiding something. i <u>was</u> hiding something.

So i started talking, just a bit. i tried to describe Rose Anna and what it was that we did together. Sort of. i didn't mention some of the feelings i was having. Also, i didn't really tell about the yard sale and the Vietnam War vet and the typewriter and the story. i mostly talked about Uncle Mo's cabin, the water and the trees, Rose Anna and me writing together. i really wanted "writing together" to be the main point.

There, i thought. i didn't have to tell you but i did. Please don't ask me too much. Please.

But then i wished i hadn't started, because she moved in with her questions. Moved right in past my main point.

"In Mo's cabin?"

"Yeah."

"Just you and a girl alone?"

"Yeah, that's what i said."

She looked away from her driving, trying to read my face. "Do you think that's a good idea, Victor?" i know she was picturing the nice soft bed up in the loft, and the birds singing and all, and mating season, and nobody else around.

i wanted to say, Yes, Mom, i think it's a <u>great</u> idea, why would i be doing it if i didn't think it was a good idea, how about you, do <u>you</u> think it's a good idea to take your eyes off the road? But that sounded kind of smart-ass. i don't do smart-ass. At least not out loud.

But see, if my mom has a strong opinion about something related to my growing up, she'll put it in the form of a question, but phrased really clever, so that i end up helplessly watching her opinion come out of <u>my</u> mouth. It's hard to explain, it's a technique she got from some book about parenting. It works but it's maddening. Sometimes i have to dig in.

"It's fine, Mom. We're just writing. She's just a friend. Can't i have a friend who's a girl?" i said that, but of course Rose Anna was more than that. i remembered the tingling in my back.

"But you're alone together. That's a Big Responsibility." She said it that way--with Big Capital Letters.

"Mom. We know."

"What did you say her name was? Roseanne?"

"Rose Anna. Rose. Anna."

"Where does she live?"

"At the bottom of South Road, near the old Franklin place. She calls it the Free Farm."

Mom nodded. Then she started her interrogation. My mom could have been a prosecutor. The kind that never gives a witness time to think. How old is she, what grade is she in, oh she doesn't go to the high school, oh, where does she-- Uh-huh, homeschooled, oh I see, well, who are her mom and dad, what kind of, oh, right, by Franklin's, the second house up on the left, I know them, actually I don't really know her father but I used to know her mother pretty well, years ago--Julia, she lived at the farm down the road from us. The big commune with lots of people.

"Maple Hill?" i asked.

"No, farther away. The Thompson Pasture. The one that had the fire. I've told you about that."

"Yeah. i've read about it too," i said.

"Then you've heard her mother mentioned. She lost her husband in the fire."

"Her husband?"

"Maybe not her real husband, but they were together. That was the saddest night. Four people died."

We were off and running on one of those commune stories my mom liked to tell and i didn't mind hearing, unless they were embarrassing. Usually it meant my part of the conversation--in this case my interrogation--was over. Or if it wasn't quite, i could push it in that direction without too much effort. i know most kids don't care that much about their parents' former lives, but i do, and anyway i'd rather talk about her life than mine. If there's a choice.

"You knew the people who died?" i said, giving that slight conversational push.

"Yes. One of them had just come back from a long trip. He was going away again. He had just hitched up there to spend one night. To say goodbye."

"Wow."

"What a shame. I saw him walk by the morning he came back. I was working in the garden, and he was headed down to the Pasture. He looked . . . jaunty. He had this old formal tuxedo shirt on, the kind with embroidery. I went out to the road to talk with him. He gave me a big hug, said he was going to Australia, or New Zealand. Just come to spend one night, he said. I'll never forget. What a night to pick. He died a few hours later."

"What happened?"

"Well, the nearest phone was a mile away. And you know the fire department; they have to call the volunteers out of bed. And it was mud season! There was nothing left when they got there. Julia and her man got out okay. What was his name? Michael: that was it. But then he ran back in. I don't know why. He was out, safe, and then he ran back in. Probably trying to save someone. He was that kind of person. We ran over as soon as we heard. We could smell it long before we got there--"

i wondered if Rose Anna knew about all this. Then i figured, of course, her mother had taken her through it and over it a hundred times, i bet.

Homeschooling.

My mom was still talking. "He's buried up there somewhere."

"What do you mean?"

"There's a law in Vermont that says you can be buried on your own land if you want to be."

"Really? Like right on your front lawn?" i could picture our five stones there, and another family arriving with a moving van. Maybe putting down the sofa and stopping to read the inscriptions on their way to the front porch.

She laughed. "No, no, just out in the country. They had a big funeral for him, and--I haven't thought about this in years-- there's this old 'debtors' graveyard' up above the Pasture, near Owl's Head. It used to be for poor people who couldn't afford being buried. I'll bet you can't even find it now. Even then, it was all overgrown like an old cellar hole, but you could still see the stone markers, just pieces of granite, no carving on them, or names."

We pulled into the driveway about then, and she turned off the car. "Spooky place," she said. "But that's where they buried him."

i wanted to get to one point before we got out of the car. "Anyway, tomorrow i'm meeting her up at the cabin."

"Who?"

"Rose Anna."

"You are?"

"Yeah. To write together."

Mom looked like she had a whole new set of questions to ask, but instead she kind of tightened her mouth and headed toward the front steps.

Hi this is Rose Anna--

That is really silly. Who am I saying hi to?

I'm up in the cabin. Victor's not here--he's in school--so I'm typing on his ROYAL--

Wait! I didn't come up on purpose to do this. Dash and I were out tracking. We came up through the woods from the east and there was the cabin looking all lonely. I even peered through the window hoping he'd skipped school or something and was in there, but no. I thought, Well, I'll go in. I worked on my story for a while. And then I realized I could do this.

My first time on the ROYAL. *#&+=%! Probably my last, too.

I bet he thinks I don't even know how to type. Like I'm so old-fashioned. His longhand pen and ink lady. Well, not his. How do you underline on this thing? _____ his. There. I know he doesn't think I'm <u>his</u> anything.

Actually I can type really fast. That's what I'm doing today: typing really really fast, to see what comes out. You know, when you write with a pen, things come out slow. Typing is more automatic. So you don't edit as much.

Victor's capital I sticks. He doesn't use it enough. I know he said he wants to stay under the radar, but give me a break. By now he should come out and capitalize. Capital I's.

That was a joke. How could the capital I be sticky if the lowercase one isn't? It <u>is</u> the same key, after all. But with the shift button depressed? Well, not depressed. I don't like that word. Pushed down.

Anyway. Capital eyes. He has those.

Victor will <u>never</u> describe himself. It's not fair. I

get described all the time, because I'm a girl and he's the Writer . . .

So I will be the Writer here. Victor has straight brown really long hair. It smells incredibly good. He's about five eight. We don't have any measuring things up here, but we stood against the cabin door post and scratched little lines above both our heads with my pocketknife. It's a Barlow. He's about three inches taller than me. And I'm five five proud. "Proud" is Vermontese for "a little more than."

I'm sure he's still got some growing to do because when I was measuring him and touched him near the waist I felt some fat there, just a little, love handles. (And, actually I did <u>see</u> them once, too.) He's modest about that, even embarrassed, but he doesn't have to be. Any teenage health book will tell you, it's stored there, the fat, horizontally, to be used up in moving vertically. You know, in growing.

I leaned against him when I went to scribe the mark over his head. Took my time. I liked that--me pressing into him and holding a knife over his head. But I think it made him nervous.

So, what does he look like? First, if you want to know anything for sure about anybody, you have to look in their eyes. Forget the rest. At least till after. His are brown, incredibly warm and gentle, but with a kind of glitter like a bit of extra intelligence. Like a sparkly stone in the trout pool.

That's what his eyes are like. Really sensitive. And it's amazing how he uses them. And his ears. He's got this totally photographic memory for detail, for things he sees and hears. He'd be a great tracker if he had some good outdoor training.

I can't believe how much I'm getting into this. He would definitely not approve. It's so <u>over</u> the radar.

What else? He smiles a lot, doesn't laugh much. Has a nice voice. Chooses his words really carefully. Care fully. He cares fully. His lips are really expressive. Made for kissing.

Mmmmmmm.

. . . . (!!) . . .

I'm back. Where were we?

Right.

I just realized what I can do. I won't show these pages to him. I'll put them in my pack, and next time we're here together I'll wait for when he's not looking. Like when he goes out to pee or something. I'll stick these pages in his pile. I don't think he ever reads his over so these'll just be in there, hidden. So like, if the whole thing ever gets read, they'll suddenly appear! But it'll be like crazy time traveling, because today is May 25, but it'll go in a couple of weeks back. I know that's hard to understand but trust me.

What else? I watch him sometimes, when he's not actually typing.

You can tell he's a touch person. He like caresses this machine. And it's so beautiful, it's got all these levers and rollers and silver buttons--he's always running his fingers over and under them, I don't even think he knows he's doing it, like he's trying to feel how much you have to push on them to get a response. And this is all while his mind is totally somewhere else.

And then, he sort of slides all his fingertips down past the space bar and sends both his arms out sideways and behind him to stretch, all the time staring at his paper, and when he's fully stretched behind he smiles, then back to the typing. Never even notices me looking.

Well, once or twice our eyes met. The first time

he put his arms out like that I wanted to get up and go put myself in them, pull his arms around me if I had to.

Don't get me wrong. I get enough love in my life, but this would be different. Anyway I didn't. It probably would be fine to do that outside under the trees, and maybe I will. In here, I think it would scare him. Like he was trapped. And I don't want to frighten him like that first time when I followed him up here. He was so scared he ran right by me! I could have stepped out and said hello but I didn't. But yes, I do think about what it would feel like--

See, I'm doing the exact thing to him that I ragged on him for doing with me. For looking at the other person that way. Sexually. It's hard not to. It's how we're programmed. Even girls. It's the culture.

I like being here with him. But I have to say I also like coming alone. Well, with Dash. We've been coming here for years. To the woods, and sometimes to the cabin. Usually, I don't want to stay away from home for too long, like for the whole day. I mean, I'm sure my mom is fine, but still.

I like to sit on the deck and work on my tracking journal. Well, it's more like a whole woods diary. I fill one up and then go buy another. With quotes from Aldo Leopold, Annie Dillard, Thoreau. And lots of tracking notes--I <u>love</u> tracking notes: like, "Saturday, April 17/ Bobcat scat on the sugarbush ledges. Found one good rear track. Bits of fur on a back-scratching rock. Dash wouldn't even go near it."

Or "Wednesday, April 21/ Something must be happening up here. Partridge thumping like a heartbeat."

Here's the one I wouldn't let him see: "Saturday, April 24, 3 p.m./ Little Acre: sighted human, male adolescent, long-haired, on silver mountain bike emerging from woods. Helmeted. Followed his trail. Gnarly tires."

I like that one. Bare bones. That's what a tracking journal is. Little bits of very important information, like a track itself. With just enough of a sign so that you can follow it. Then, later, if you want to fill in more detail, you can.

So, let's fill in that last entry.

Some poor animal up in the pasture had gotten a faceful of quills, and I was trying to figure out who, meditating in my tracker's head, that's what you do when you try to take your mind down to a deeper level. Dash has learned to be totally quiet with me while I'm tracking. He won't even bark if a bull moose walks by. That happened once.

Anyway, I was just getting the picture, maybe a young coyote who didn't know better, when wham, a bike came hurtling through the opening in the stone wall-- I mean he was so close but he didn't even see us. He just sped by.

We just sat there in the weeds till he was gone. He hit the road by Franklin's barn, never looked back, and turned left.

So then, of course, I followed <u>his</u> track. Not where he was going. His back track, into the woods.

The first thing I found was that the tire tracks ended really soon. So he must have parked the bike. His feet led away uphill. Funny, the trail's not that steep. I couldn't figure why he stopped riding. His footprints were right there easy to follow. But they were really strange. Not like a normal male teenage human. For one thing, the stride was really short, feet close together. All his weight was on his heels. Looked like old shoes. I was glad the ground was soft. I was learning so much. But I was really puzzled. At one point I stopped and meditated about it. And then I thought: Got it! He's carrying something! Something heavy.

Ooooh, I thought, this is getting interesting. Treasure? A dead body? He was empty-handed when he came out.

I started picking up the rest of the story. There was one place, and then another, where he stopped and sat down. You could see the two prints together where he stood back up from resting on a big hollow log just off-trail. And one snapped-off hazel seedling about ankle level. Dash found that and took a good sniff at it. Was he going to the cabin? I knew someone else besides me goes there sometimes, but I've never seen him. Now I thought maybe I'd found him. Couldn't figure out what he was carrying, though.

The cabin, that's where he went. Through the sugarbush and up and over the knoll. There were his footprints on the three steps up to the deck. Nearly dried now. I peeked in the window: mystery of the funny walk solved!

I said, Dash, look at that big thing he lugged in! Of course, Dash couldn't see inside. He doesn't even come up to the window. So I lifted his front legs and put them on the sill so he could look in.

That's when I decided I'd watch for when he came back. I knew it'd be soon. You don't lug a big typewriter up like that and then just leave it.

I'm going to stop now. I really only wanted to fill in a few gaps in his story and test-drive the ROYAL myself. Smooth ride. Fast.

You're a nice machine but you'll never take the place of good old pen and ink--Wiccan ink. At least not for me. Ink with my Granma's spell on it. Spelling in ink. You use witch ink, ma'am? Yes.

Dash is pacing around out there. He's not barking but he's nervous.

I'd better get dressed.

16

May 15

Saturday. Rose Anna and me at the cabin. Today we have a good long time. No family trip or anything. No hurry. We write a little bit, and then Rose Anna shows me a part of her story i haven't seen yet. i know when she was writing it--yesterday while i was riding in the car with my mom, having a conversation i wished i hadn't started.

There's a kind of ratty--i mean mousy--sofa near the table. We sit next to each other and read together.

The three newts are crossing a meadow with no cover. They keep glancing up at the sky, all of them afraid of what might swoop down and eat them. Then a long-necked heron's shadow moves over the ground. Wings flapping slow, the shadow rippling over high and low places. They all cringe as the shadow passes right over them, and they hear the heron's long-throat call. There's no other birdcall like it.

After it goes by, they stop and suck rainwater from a patch of moss. There's a box turtle and lots of little insects flying in tight formation over the wet place, like a traveling air show.

Oona keeps noticing Solemn Andrew. He smiles at her but she can tell his mind is somewhere else. The Summit Meeting, probably, she thinks, and wonders what it's all about.

In late afternoon they come to an old barbed-wire fence. There are twigs and dry grass and dirty old spiderwebs hanging from it.

Crawling under the rusty wire, Oona scrapes herself. "Oh. Ow."

Newts' backs are tender. Solemn Andrew, twice her size, never comes close to the wire. He seems to ooze under it, flat as if a child's paintbrush had painted him there. A shiny black, spotted lizard. Amoss figures out his own way to deal with the fence. He loops his tail on the wire above and swings right through the gap.

Show-off, Oona thinks.

Big trees are all around them. As the forest gets dark, it's as if every shadow holds eyes looking at them, every sound seems directed their way.

They hide under an old fallen tree trunk. It's half rotten and full of moss and fungi and crawling things. Just like home. All around them, all the sounds and sights of nighttime approaching. Moths fluttering by. Friendly bird couples roosting in the maples. Tiny glowing spots of fox fire start to come on above them in the rotting wood. Behind Oona Newt, the sky turns flaming.

"It's not hard to see why people think of you and fire in the same breath," Solemn Andrew says.

Her eyes flash. "Me and fire?"

"Red salamanders and fire. They go together."

Oona's never seen a fire. All she knows about fire comes from family legends meant to frighten her. Now all those stories crowd

into her mind, and she can almost hear the crackling of flames.
But it cross-fades to another sound that's real and right next to
her ear: Amoss is chewing a tasty wintergreen leaf, like an after-
dinner mint. Loudly. "Solemn Andrew is going to tell us a story. I
can always tell," he says. Then he crunches some more.

That's it. i look up. Rose Anna's watching me. i'm distracted today.

First of all, sitting on the sofa with her. It's so saggy, it's impossible for two bodies to stay apart. We keep knocking together.

Another thing is, i keep thinking i shouldn't have told my mom yesterday, about Rose Anna. When i left this morning, my mom looked worried, like, What could happen up there when we had a whole day together? So, knowing my mom, she might head up here just to check things out. And drag Claire along as an excuse.

"What?" Rose Anna asks. As if i've said something. i must have some strange expression on my face.

"Nothing."

But i could just as easily have said "What?" to her. She looks bothered, too.

The third thing that's distracting me--that's what Rose Anna picks up on. "You still having trouble with the newts?" she says.

i nod my head, but just slightly. It's not a strong feeling. And, you know, it's her writing and i don't have the right to influence it.

She's quiet for a while. "You think i should forget fantasy and just write about people?"

i shake my head. Whether or not i think so, that's completely up to her. It's her choice.

She gets up. i felt that coming. She starts moving around the cabin. The forest is out there humming, and it's hard for both of us to just sit, inside. That's another distraction.

When we're here, we're careful not to move around too much. Like, if we just sit and get mental with each other, then we won't get physical. Now it's like she's changing the game. She stretches. She knows i'm watching her but she ignores that.

i keep looking, and i want to touch her. But i don't. i want to tell her all i'm feeling. But i'll write it instead, she'll find out when she reads. i don't make the first move. My first move is typing.

She doesn't sit back down after stretching. She's pacing now, looking past me out the window at the brook and the trees. Something's making her jumpy.

"Maybe I should just tell you this part of the story?" she asks. "Out loud?"

"If you want."

"Do you take dictation?" She says it with a laugh.

"Sure. If that's part of the job."

"Great." She points. "Why don't you move over there?"

i get up to carry the ROYAL around to her side so i can type and watch her at the same time. Its rubber pads stick to the table like it's dug in now and doesn't want to move. Afraid i'm going to haul it back to the old guy's basement. No way, man, i told you this was the end of the line.

Damn. Forgot how heavy it was. How'd i carry it all the way up here?

Rose Anna is standing under the loft, waiting. We never use the rest of the downstairs. With the open space between the woodstove and the kitchen cabinets, and the hemlock beam overhead, it's like a little theater.

If i could change the type font, i would, but you can't on an old ROYAL. So it's going to look like everything else i've written.

"Ready when you are," i go.

She breathes out. Warming up for storytelling. She makes circles with her neck, which makes her hair frizz out. "All right--wait--don't! Please don't describe me, okay?"

"Don't describe you?"

"You were describing me just now, weren't you?"

"Well, yeah--"

"Please. Just type what I <u>say</u>. Not how I look. You've described me enough anyway. I'll never be able to walk down Main Street again. Everyone's going to know everything about me."

i'm not planning to leaflet the town. But i guess i could. Staple it up on telephone poles. Have you seen this person? No, no, it's not that she's missing, i just think you should know all this cool stuff about her.

"Okay?" she insists. "Just the story, nothing else."

"Okay, but i may say something too, or add some thoughts of my own--"

"Fair enough. You ready?"

"Ready."

She begins again. "Okay. Oh, wait. Can I explain something first?"

"Yes."

"This whole story is about signs."

"Signs?"

"Yes, but not the little signs you see if you're a tracker, like paw prints, or poop, bites out of a mushroom. Big signs: that's where I'm going even if you think I'm taking way too much time to get there."

"i didn't say anything."

"No but you were thinking it. I could tell."

"Whatever."

"Big signs--earthquakes or eclipses or tsunamis. Like when you're in a huge thunderstorm and some god is trying to get your attention--"

i nod. i've been in storms like that. Once in a canoe. Out in the open.

"Oh, and totem animals," she says. "Do you know about them?"

"No."

"There's books about them, or you can go online. Each of the cardinal elements has an animal. A spirit animal. You know what the four elements are, don't you?"

Finally something i do know. "Sure. Earth, water, fire, and wind."

"Air."

"That's what i meant. Air."

"Everybody has a totem animal. Mine's a salamander. I was born with what my dad calls 'newt-consciousness,' which means that when we go walking, I see one before anyone else does, bright red like my T-shirts. I knew they were my animal even before I knew they were the totem of fire."

Rose Anna's really getting into telling me all this. She's using the space, like they say in soccer. She's moving her hands and her eyes like a magician, pretending there's this little newt crawling across her palms. She bends over--whoops, i'm not supposed to describe her.

"They really tickle you when they walk on your hands. They'll try to get away, but you can trick them by switching hands--they keep going cause they think they're getting somewhere, even though they're not. They're so beautiful, you wouldn't want to harm them. So when you're done, you put them down somewhere safe. We'll have to come up here sometime when it's raining, that's when they all come out."

"They like water?"

"Yeah."

"So why aren't they water totems?"

"I don't know. Some alchemist in the Middle Ages was probably doing some nasty fire experiment once and thought he saw one crawling out alive. Plus a lot of them look like flame."

"Neat."

"Also, I should tell you," she says, so quietly i almost can't hear her, "I have a thing about fire."

"i know," i say, but then i wish i hadn't.

"You know?"

"All right, i don't know, but, yesterday, with my mom's story about the Thompson Pasture fire and all, i just figured, you know . . ."

i let it go. i said a while ago that i could read the tracks that thoughts leave on a face. Just then, her face had so many--it was like a water hole in a drought and every single animal comes, and every footprint stomps over the last one, and in the end you can't read a thing.

I wait. "Are you gonna tell it?" i ask.

"Tell what?"

"Your story."

She shakes her head. "No."

"Okay."

"Yes," she says. "Please just listen, all right?"

"All right then."

"You remember where I was?"

"Yeah. The solemn guy was about to tell a story. A story within a story."

She shushes me with her finger. "The three newts draw closer under the log, so Solemn Andrew can whisper. They have no real enemies in the forest, but still, you can't be sure. Oona's eyes are all crimson, the reflection of the sky, and that's where we see Solemn Andrew and Amoss, black silhouettes in her eyes.

"Solemn Andrew says: A long time ago, in the beginning of the world, before everything got all mixed up together, there were only four separate elements: earth, water, fire, and air. Victor thinks it's wind, but it's air."

"Hey. Stick to the story."

"Shut up. How the four elements got here, nobody knows. But they remained for thousands of lifetimes, never changing.

Amoss goes, Wow, is that true?

And Oona says: Shhhhh.

And Solemn Andrew says, Eventually, inside of each element, one animal began to grow. We call them totem animals. Where they came from, nobody knows. What they look like, also, no one agrees. But over the course of thousands more lifetimes--"

My wrists are starting to cramp. And i have to change the paper.

"Slow down," i tell her. "i'm actually trying to get this all down." Trouble is, Rose Anna doesn't pause that much when she talks.

"--over the course of thousands more lifetimes, the animals sent copies of themselves out to mix with each other. Thousands of new species of animals, combinations of earth, water, air, and fire, were formed, and started traveling around. But deep within each of the four elements those four original totem animals remained, never changing. Would you like to know their names?"

--"Are you asking me?" i say--

"Shhhh. Amoss and Oona answer together: Yes, tell us.

And Solemn Andrew says, The totem animal of earth is called a gnome. Of water, the undine. Of air, the sylph. Of fire, the salamander.

Oona whispers: That's us! We see her shiver, although I don't know whether salamanders can shiver. But her eyes get really wide.

He goes on: Now, of all of the mixtures of earth, water, fire, and air, out here and traveling around, the most complicated is called 'the human being.'

And Amoss sighs: I knew that's where this story was heading.

And Solemn Andrew says: No other animal calls itself 'a being.'

Oona and Amoss creep closer to Solemn Andrew in the darkness. He is even quieter now, as if speaking about humans suddenly makes everything scary--

Then, they almost jump out of their skins! A big owl lands right on their log--bits of wood shower down, you can see his huge claws dig in right over their heads. They gleam in the moonlight. Like murder weapons! Put an exclamation point there."

"i did!"

"The owl rests for a moment and then flies off. Solemn Andrew can hardly speak, but he pushes on: We are the only totem animals that human beings have ever actually seen for more than an instant! The others can appear suddenly, but if you rub your eyes, or look away for a moment, then look back, they're gone. Their tracks are hard to follow because they're only in your mind. When they appear to humans, it's always when the humans need help.

When they need help? Oona asks.

Yes, he says, that's when the totem animals appear.

Do they need help now?

Yes, he says. That's what the meeting's about. We're all going to be there!

Who?

The elementals, my dear--

Then he says, real dramatically: I have seen the other three, once before.

And Amoss and Oona go, You have?

Well, I've only seen a picture of them, in an old, old book I found. In the ruins of a house that burned down years ago. You'll see the place. We have to go right by there tomorrow--

Oona says, We do?

Her eyes get wider, and where before there was red sky reflected in them, now it's real fire--it jumps in out of nowhere, already at its peak with flames roaring--and Solemn Andrew is saying, totally burned! Four human beings burned up, too . . .

It's all in Oona's eyes, close up. She's blinking fast, trying not to see it, but it doesn't go away! I mean she's just found out that she's the totem of fire, she is fire, the cause of every fire, and they have to walk right by the ruins tomorrow, and now, she can't stop seeing it, she can't, can't--"

Rose Anna stops talking. Just like that. "That's enough," she says.

"But what happens next?"

"I don't know."

"You don't know? It's your story."

"Guess we'll find out next time. Did you get it all?"

"More or less."

"Thanks," she says. She steps out from under the loft and grabs her backpack, throws her pen, ink, and paper in. "Let's go." No warning, she's suddenly in a hurry to leave. It's still early. i thought we were going to spend all day--

i don't know what to say.

Her eyes look dark, but not dark like some deep inviting pool. Dark like a curtain.

i lug the ROYAL back to its usual spot. Get the paper ready for another day. Clean up. i'm doing the whole ceremony my-self. She just stands at the door waiting for me.

When we leave, she asks, "Did you like it?" But i feel like all of a sudden she doesn't care, she's just making an effort to be friendly. i want to reach her somehow. i've been waiting for the right time to hold her hand. i tell myself, Do it now. Make the move.

i do. But it feels like there's no one attached to it. She doesn't even look at me.

17

May 18

After the last time at the cabin, i didn't know how i felt about going there again. i was wondering, Will she act like nothing happened? Will she even be there? i didn't ride as fast as usual.

Rose Anna was sitting at Mo's trailhead, so we had a long time to look at each other while i crossed the field. She reached for my hand right away. She was quiet on the walk up, like last time. But at least it felt like this hand was connected to somebody.

When she's that quiet, it's usually because she's concentrating on her tracking. So i get quiet, too, and think too much, or listen to the sounds we make walking. But this time was different--she was somewhere else. She kept squeezing my hand, and after a while it felt rhythmical, like she was singing a song or something in her head, and the hand squeeze was the beat that went with it.

Up at the cabin, i did all the opening and setting up. i decided to get right to work, like if i acted normal, she would, too. i typed for a while, then all of a sudden i stopped. Rose

Anna still looked as if her mind was miles away. Her pen was lying on the table. Her pages were blank. Her eyes were blank, too.

"What's up?"

"Not much," she said. She tried to push her mouth up into a smile, but gravity took over and it didn't go anywhere. Certainly not up.

"You want to tell me?" i asked. A voice inside me said, Go over to her. But another voice said, Just sit and listen.

"No," she said.

"Okay."

"Yes."

"Okay."

"Should I start at the beginning?"

"i guess. If you want to."

"I do."

"Okay."

"Stop saying okay!"

"Okay."

She glared at me. "Do you ever wonder why I don't go to school?"

"Yeah--"

"Well, it's only my theory. I mean if you were to ask my parents, they'd say it's because public education sucks. One day in third grade I brought home some homework assignment, color this flag and fill in the blank words, that was so stupid, so dumbed-down, that they yanked me out of Pine Street School the next day and I haven't gone back. Ever."

"Is that how it happened?" i asked her.

"Maybe, I don't really remember. But see, the real reason I

don't know what actually happened is that I've heard that story too many times. So now I think, it's just what they say, to cover up the truth."

"Which is?"

"I think the truth is that my mom was so depressed that my dad decided I'd better stay home with her, give her something to do--my education, for instance--to keep her from killing herself while she's home alone."

"Wow! Would she really do that?"

"No. I mean I don't think so. No. A lot of depressed people do, but I don't think she would."

"Can't they just give her some kind of pill?" i asked.

"Not my mom. She doesn't take pills."

"Oh."

"Yeah. Well, she takes some. Vitamins and herbs and things, you know, Saint John's Warts or whatever, ginko, but that's all."

"Well, you like being homeschooled, don't you?" i said. "And you know more than anyone. Especially about cool stuff we don't get to study."

"Still, it's only the two of us, day after day, and that's not a good thing. That's why Dash and me come up here a lot. Sometimes we have to get out of there--it's like what she has is contagious--"

"Rose Anna," i said really fast, "i don't think so."

i said that, but suddenly i was afraid that depression <u>could</u> be contagious. That it <u>can</u> sneak up on people and change them in front of your eyes. Even people who seemed totally normal a minute ago. i mean, look how she'd been acting lately.

"Well, maybe not," she said, "but the worst thing is, I feel like I'm the reason she's depressed. At least part of it."

i couldn't believe she said that. i couldn't think of any way Rose Anna could be the cause of anyone's depression, anywhere, anytime. No way. Not unless she turned her back on them and walked out of their life. Out of their log cabin.

"--And your reason is . . . ?" i said.

"Don't laugh at me."

"Of course not."

"Okay. One of the things that can happen when you're an only child, and homeschooled, is that you can think of yourself as somehow different."

"i've heard that. So?"

"Well, even before I was homeschooled, I always felt different. That I was special. I don't mean bragging special. I don't mean that at all. I'm not spoiled if that's what you're thinking."

"i'm not thinking that."

"Good. But when I was very young, I used to think that the only reason my mom and dad met was so I could get born. For no other reason. It was very important that I get born."

"It was," i said. "Who would i write with if you weren't here?"

"Victor--" she started, and her voice had a strange new tone. "Are you serious?"

"No," i said, quickly.

"Cause if you are, you can take a hike. You are not the reason that I exist."

"i know."

She kind of glared at me. "Women don't exist _for_ men."

"i was just kidding."

She ignored that and went on. At least she let me stay in her cabin.

"The problem was," she said, "I couldn't get born. Rose Anna. This particular gene combination. Because my mom was with someone else. His name was Michael."

"i know about him, my mother told me. He died in a fire."

"In the fire," she corrected me.

"The fire. Whatever."

"It's not whatever. My mom dates absolutely everything in her whole life from that fire, before it and after it. She's never gotten over it. And it was my fault."

"Rose Anna--"

"Let me finish! Not totally my fault. Just partly. Like, God needs Rose Anna to be born, to Julia and my dad, but he's not even in the picture yet. But she's not about to split up with this guy she's with. So one night He, or She, decides to bring a case of cheap wine to this hippie farm Julia lives at, which is hard cause it's the middle of mud season and they have to go in and out on foot, and there's rules against drinking, written up on the wall, cause it's a commune where strangers come in and crash all the time, and they need to know the rules, but somehow the wine gets there, and then, in order for the plan, His or Her plan, to work, people have to get drunk and go up-stairs and screw each other in the dark and pass out--and downstairs someone falls asleep and knocks over a candle, maybe that guy you say your mom met who only came back for a night, he's the one who did it, maybe that's why he was sent back, to accidentally kill this guy Michael, in the fire, who Julia loves more than anything in the world--"

"Wow. What was he like?"

"I don't know. I never met him. He <u>died</u>." She stood up quickly, knocking over her chair.

"i know," i said, reaching out for her. But she was too quick for me. She rushed out the screen door and along the deck.

i caught up to her at the top of the steps, and we both leaned against the deck rail. i wanted to hold on to her, but i didn't know where to touch her. She was in this state, and going somewhere in it, somewhere important. If i touched her the wrong way, it would stop her--

She was staring straight ahead. "Everyone I've ever asked about him says: Oh, he was the neatest, the most gentle, he was so gorgeous, a woodsman, acrobat, dancer, incredibly wise. He was always my mom's first love, and because God just ripped him away from her in the flames that morning, she's never really given him up."

"That's not very fair to your dad," i said.

"Tell me about it," she said. "And it's my fault."

"It's not your fault," i told her.

"It is!" she said. "I just explained it to you. You weren't even listening!"

"i <u>was</u>."

"I told you. I had to get born somehow. It's creepy. I know my dad is my dad, but sometimes it's like he's not, cause my mom is so stuck back then, I see her looking right through him, and me, trying to see this man step out of the fire, see all these children she could have had with him--"

"That doesn't make sense," i started to say.

"I know, it's sick. Sometimes I start to think I really was there and I was the only one who got rescued--"

She moved from the porch rail and sat down on the top step. i followed her. She actually started to cry then, really cry, like she'd been holding it in for a while. Nobody ever told me what to do when someone right next to you starts to cry like that. Especially a woman or a girl.

i sat there squeezing her. It felt like nothing i had any relation to, in my own life. i don't think i've cried like that since i was about five. She was like an engine that was revving too hard, and i couldn't find the stop button. All i could do was hold on and wait.

Finally she began to speak. "Why did it have to be so messy? I know God has to get people out of the way sometimes, but he never never does it easy, he sends stuff like fires or train wrecks or galloping pneumonia--"

"What's that?"

"It's some bacteria that starts in your chest and clogs your breath and kills you in about two days. You burn up with a fever and suffocate. That <u>Muppets</u> guy died of it."

"Oh."

She went on. "Or concrete blocks falling off of building ledges and crushing your head while you're just walking down the street, or a boat suddenly flipping over in a freak wind and you get caught underneath and drown, or some crazy loner guy walks into your school and shoots you, or some drunk driver smashes into your bike, or you back up your truck into a farm pond, or some--"

"Stop it!" i said. "Enough!"

We almost had a fight then, a physical fight. She was crying again now, we were trying to grab each other's wrists, i don't know why. Fighting. Us.

It was like she needed to wrestle with something, someone, and i just happened to be there--the nearest living thing. We were pulling at each other, touching, grabbing, poking each other like we never had before, <u>where</u> we never had before, i was under and then i was over, our faces were against each other, in another few seconds we would be on the ground at the bottom of the three steps, rolling around in the grass and the wild strawberries, but that wouldn't be good, i thought, we wouldn't stop, wouldn't know how to stop, we wouldn't even know what we were doing--

i pulled back, i sat still. i forget exactly what i said; it all spilled out of me. i told her she was crazy, no, she was <u>not</u> crazy, that was the point, maybe her mother was crazy but <u>she</u> wasn't, not even close to it! i didn't care what her element was, she had absolutely nothing to do with that fire; it happened ten years before she was even born--and she went yes that's how you think but that's cause you're you, and you're a guy, guys have such a screwed up linear notion of time!

She was almost sobbing again. "How do you know I wasn't there? Not my body, my <u>design</u>. Don't you know about chaos theory? What proof do you have?"

i left her and ran into the cabin, and then came right back out.

"Look at this." i showed her an old calendar that was still on the wall because my uncle Mo had kept it--he liked the old photos of the southwest Indians, Navajos and Hopis, with their furs and long rifles and the incredible deep wrinkles on their faces--

"See? Twelve months, one after another. Nineteen eighty-five. January to December. Those months are never going to come again. That was then. And we weren't even born yet. You weren't there."

"How can you dare," she said, grabbing the calendar and waving it at me, swatting the air right in front of my face, "to use this as an example of linear time? Go read any book of Hopi stories: it's all circles. Their <u>time</u> is circles circles circles; their cause and effect is circular! I could have gone back and been there as sure as I'm right here, you're so--pedestrian. You are such a straight line!"

"Like my story?" i asked. i gripped her wrist really hard to make her stop waving the calendar at me--

"Yes, exactly like your story," she shot back, loud and mean. Immediately i saw the reaction in her face; i must have looked so hurt.

"No I'm sorry I didn't mean that. It came out wrong. I love your story."

"Right," i said.

"I do!"

"Sure."

"<u>I</u> <u>do!</u> And it has to be told the way you're telling it, no other way. It's so you--and I love you."

"You what?" i said.

"I love you," she repeated. She stood there totally facing me like she had nothing to hide.

"Wow."

"Is that all you can say?" she said.

"Wow."

"You said that already. Say something else."

"i love you, too."

She looked for a moment like she didn't know what i meant. At the same time, i was wondering where those words had come from.

She took a step closer to me. "Couldn't you take off the 'too' so it's not like you're just saying it because I said it? Don't say it like you're only saying it cause you have to."

But i looked away, and sat down on the top step and stared up toward the trail. i was stunned by what had just come out of me. i took in a breath as if i was going to speak, but nothing came out.

She waited, and then came around, sat on the step below me, and pushed her back against me. i took that to mean she forgave me for not repeating it.

"So we agree about one thing," she said.

"We agree about lots of things," i pointed out.

"You don't do capital I's."

"Maybe i will someday. Anyway, sometimes i do. Just not about me."

She snorted, and wiped her nose on her sleeve.

We just sat. She was leaning back into me, and i was sitting behind her, my chest pressed against her back, my legs and arms wrapped around her tight. We were breathing together. It felt so good to have my mouth and nose and eyes buried in all that hair. It was like i had never smelled anything before in my whole life. Not like this.

Ten steps away from us, the stream kept chattering down between the stones. When i looked up, all these beautiful new spring leaves were dancing around in the trees above us. Poplars and maples and silver birches.

Dash came over and lay down, pressed against my back. The three of us sat there. The ROYAL and the paper and the gold pen were all inside on the table. Waiting.

Finally Rose Anna started to stretch and get up.

"That felt really good," she said.

"What did?" i asked.

"All of it."

18

Back inside, we sat down. She was finally about to get to work, and then she looked up and said, "You know what?"

"What?"

"I'm not writing a story anymore."

"You're not?" That scared me. Were we going to stop writing together?

"No. It's a movie. It'll be up on a big screen, with lots of people sitting in the dark watching it."

"How will you get the lizards to act?" i asked. i like to get her upset, calling them lizards.

"They're animated. Everything'll be drawn."

"Oh. Cool." And then i said, "Do you know how to do that?"

She put on this expression of surprise. "Sure. Doesn't everybody?"

It's early morning.

Oh, Oona realizes, I must have fallen asleep. The log over her head is still there in the same exact place, but it's just a big old rotten log, no moonlight or fox fire on it, no sharp owl claws.

The first movement we see is long fingers of pink mist slowly swirling into the film frame and blowing by, then Oona's head poking up through the mist.

Then we see what she sees.

Morning dew sparkling on everything that can hold it—the old fence wire, twigs, ferns, trembling spiderwebs. It's as if the three of them had wandered the night before into a treasure room but didn't know it, and now at first light they wake up surrounded by jewels. Oona doesn't even have to move to quench her morning thirst. Then she turns and watches Solemn Andrew.

He comes out from under the log and lifts his head to the east, sniffing. He moves away and half disappears in a bright patch of wintergreen. We see him raise himself on all four legs and breathe out. Then he turns around and comes back, leaving behind the smallest golden drop of liquid on the pine needles, a little wisp of steam rising from it. Although newt pee is probably not actually warm.

Meanwhile, Amoss wakes up next to Oona and starts thrashing around, whipping his long tail back and forth and pumping up and down on his front legs, making a big show of his energy. Morning exercises. Push-ups. Newt yoga. Salamander Sun Salute. Upward-facing Newt.

"Boys," Oona whispers.

Solemn Andrew comes back and looks at each of them, deep into their eyes. Just like he did yesterday.

"We have no time to waste," he says.

He turns his head to indicate where Owl's Head is, but it's completely hidden behind the trees.

"We have to get up there before sundown," he says, already setting off. "The others will be waiting."

19

Two days can seem like a long time if you've just been through a lot with someone and they're not around to talk about it. i felt different. i was sure something had changed, but i wasn't sure what.

i came home from school. i'm always the first one home, so i usually bring in the mail. i don't know why i bother bringing it in. It's mostly junk mail, and there's never anything addressed to me. But that day there was. A small envelope. Made, not bought. You know, the kind that's just folded-up paper with lots of tape on it. The address isn't in the right place, and it's probably hard for the mailman to read because of the extra squiggles in the writing.

i recognized the pen. And the handwriting.

i took my time opening the letter. Sitting at the kitchen table with the afternoon light coming in.

Suddenly i felt afraid. Something unexpected comes in the mail like that, you know who it's from, and you've just been with them, and maybe you heard stuff you weren't supposed to hear, or feelings got too intense, or something happened, or almost happened. Did i say or do something that was over some line, inappropriate? i didn't know.

i got this twisted feeling in my stomach. My heart was racing. Did the note say she didn't want to see me anymore, didn't want to meet there ever again? Suddenly i was absolutely sure that was what it did say, and i didn't want to read it.

But i did.

It was a thank-you note.

> *Thanks for what you did.*
> *Thanks for what you didn't. I*
> *Owe you. See you soon.*

It was a haiku. Like we did in Miss Roth's class. Seventeen syllables. Five-seven-five.

What did i do? Or didn't?

i headed upstairs to hide the letter, happy i got home first, so i didn't have to explain it to anyone else. i stopped at that kitchen mirror on the way up. Did i look different? i mean, could anyone tell by looking at me what was going on? It's funny, to think that what you're absolutely sure everyone can see may not show at all.

i didn't know what she meant by "I owe you." But i realized what she meant by "soon." She meant next Wednesday. We always decide when the next time's going to be.

On the way upstairs, i wrote a haiku, too.

> *My heart beat so fast*
> *it made my brain forget things*
> *it should remember.*

20

May 26

We were sitting with our feet in the stream. We had the whole day. There was some kind of state teachers' convention, and they had set the students loose. Lucky for me, Claire stayed over at a friend's house, otherwise it'd have been me taking care of her, when all i wanted was to be up here with Rose Anna.

i felt like something good could happen if we had a whole day together. Things were different, not like the last time i thought we'd have all day--

So now we were sitting about a hundred feet downhill from the cabin. That part of the stream is almost a pool. It flows through, but slowly. There are some big silver birches there, right by the water, leaning on each other while they take a long drink.

"It's my favorite spot--" she said when she pulled me down there.

We swept the old leaves and sticks out of the pool, so the water could flow through faster. It was maybe six inches deep and about the size of a big bathtub. There were flecks of something shiny on the bottom, and you could pretend they were gold, but when you fished them out and held them up to the light, you could see they were just chips of mica.

"--and this is my favorite thing to do here," she said. She took off her sandals and put her feet in the water, up to her ankles. i did, too. We both gasped. It was cold!

Rose Anna was wearing this buckskin jacket that had fringe all over the sleeves. She had cut it off short and made new fringes all around the waist. She had on the same red T-shirts she was wearing before. The same colored beads. i bet she never took those off. Her jeans were full of big holes, loose threads, and big faded blotches. They were more white than blue.

She looked so relaxed with her feet in the water, half lying back against a big rock, curls spreading out against the rock face, i felt incredibly sorry that i hadn't been there to sit next to her all the times she must have come up here alone and decided this was her favorite place. Where was i and what was i doing all those times? i wanted--

"Aren't you going to read?" she said.

"Right. Sorry."

That was what we had come down to the stream to do.

It's full morning now.

Oona is happy. She's stepping off into a land she doesn't know. Her favorite thing to do. With two new friends who include her like she's always been part of their adventure.

Step. Happiness. Happiness. Step.

There's a voice-over. It's Oona thinking: I wonder what's around that curve? What does a burnt-out building smell like?

How does it feel to be on top of a mountain? What kind of help do the humans need? What will the other totem animals look like?

All these questions make Oona's brain dance like it did when the waterfall used to pound the top of her head. Her walk has a snap it never had before. Her four feet move in such a rhythm of joy, it makes her long tail pulse and whip in time. Amoss, right behind, has to get out of the way!

He catches up to her and they walk side by side. He seems to understand everything she's thinking, and smiles. They hustle together to keep up with Solemn Andrew, who, though slow-moving, has a longer stride. He leads the way with surprising ease.

They walk for a while through a patch of ferns soaking with dew, and the camera shows the three friends from different angles, from above, from ahead, from behind, or reflected in a dewdrop as they pass by.

Suddenly they're out of the forest, on the edge of a pasture. On the far side, looming through the mist, is a hill.

Solemn Andrew: "Here's where they had their garden."

Oona: "Who?"

Solemn Andrew: "The People. They did it wrong. They didn't know that the soil was too acid and thin. They never learned how to make it grow food. They plowed it all up and never smoothed it out before they left. It's going to be a rough walk across."

The old salamander is right. The old garden is wind-eroded, baked hard. Because of what the humans did, their journey is more difficult. They climb up mounds and tumble into furrows. Then pick themselves up and keep going. Over ground so bare, with sharp rocks sticking up, that should have been buried all easy and smooth under native grass and wildflowers.

There's an ominous feeling about the place. Like ghosts are there. Oona's mood changes, too.

Solemn Andrew says, "Their plow didn't do all this. The glacier did a lot. Thousands of years ago."

They're standing right beside where the glacier had ground down a whole mountain to half its original height. It's an old battlefield of granite gravel and crumbs of sparkly quartz and mica. I guess we know who won the fight, cause Owl's Head— what's left of it—is still up there, and the glacier's gone.

When they're almost across to the far side of the Pasture, Oona stops. Amoss and Solemn Andrew keep on going, but she stops.

We see her from above, bright red-orange against a big black patch. It's the burnt-out house, the ruin where people died. They're crossing it. But Oona can't move. She stands there looking at the charred black rectangle. Just then a wind blows through with an unpleasant sound. It moves the mist around.

Oona can't budge from that place where the fire hit. Solemn Andrew said she was the totem animal of fire. The idea scares her. The place scares her. How can it keep the shape of the house after all these years? She thinks she can still see the wooden walls and the roof, the flames reaching up to the nearby treetops—

Then Oona has a full-out vision, stronger than the night before—the sight and sound of real fire, and it's all around her; she's right in the middle but not burning up herself. We get the shrieks of the humans caught upstairs, everyone choking on superheated air, windows shattering, wine bottles exploding, and other humans outside in a mad imitation of a dance, circling the burning building, screaming.

How does she know how it looked and sounded? She wasn't there! But she was, if she is fire—

She can't move. Her mind fills with flame, beating in and out of her head. But she tries to shake it, pound it out! What does that fire, any fire, have to do with her? Her life? Whose idea is all this anyway? What do they want from her?

The thing is, she's standing totally still. Not even a twitch. It's all in her mind, although we can see and hear it.

Amoss comes back into the black rectangle and tugs at her. "Come on, Oona. We have to keep up."

She looks at him almost without seeing him.

He tugs again, and Oona pulls herself out of her daze and looks around. The fire is out. It's morning, many years after all of that happened, and they still have a hill to climb.

She smiles at him and says, "Sorry. Lead on."

He looks at her like he can't possibly know everything that's in her mind. But he would like to try.

Again, i was held back by the deal we made. i really wanted to talk about what Rose Anna had just written. But i needed to show her that i could keep my word, so i just looked up and said nothing.

"Keep my word" is such a strange expression. At first glance, it just means "Be true to what you agreed on." But it could also mean, "Hold your words back." Keep them in. Let your actions speak instead.

i wanted to act. Rose Anna was lying back again against the rock. i wanted to reach for her. But she started to talk.

"My problem is, all these years, I've been living with a lunatic."

"Who?"

"My mom. She's a moon bug. A luna tick. Get it?"

"Yeah. Is she really?"

"Yes. She knows the names of all the full moons in the year. You know, the Frost Moon, the Wolf Moon. The Flower Moon--that's the one we just had."

"i didn't know they all had names," i said.

"Most people don't. But my family <u>observes</u> them. Remember the boy band *NSYNC? You could call my family Outta Sync. We're out of sync with the whole country. In almost every way. We don't celebrate any of the holidays normal people celebrate. We do Earth Day, and May Day, only she calls it Beltane. What else? El Día de los Muertos is really big in our house."

"Day of the Dead?"

"Yeah. November second. She hangs cartoon skeletons all over the living room. From Mexico. The kind that dance when you jiggle them. They're some of my earliest memories. Some kids have colored plastic animals, I had skeletons jiggling over my head. I liked the one playing the accordion. He had the wickedest grin."

"Like this?" i asked, grinning.

"--Or the lady with the big skirt. I'd always lift it up to see underneath. It was just bones."

i laughed, because i used to like to do that, with dolls. See what they had up there. Didn't know girls did that too.

"Yeah. But it's the personal family holidays that she really gets into. She even had this huge ritual for me with all her women friends when I started, you know--"

"What?"

"When I got my first period. Bled. Became a woman."

i looked at her. i hadn't thought of her as a woman. Well no, i had, but without all the actual physical details.

i tried not to picture the Anatomy Facts she was referring to. Images came into my mind but i tried to bump them right back out. It's one thing to talk about body parts and what they can do in a health class with old Mr. Holmes, the JV soccer coach, but it was different sitting in the woods, just her and me together.

Two bodies, next to each other, with parts.

But i liked the idea of the celebration. i'd read about things like that in Will's anthropology books. Primitive tribes holding a big feast when a girl turns that corner in her life, women chanting and dancing around, showing off the evidence. Eating special ceremonial foods--red fruit, red wine. i pictured it with Rose Anna at the center.

i'll admit i was envious. i wished my dad and his friends had given me a party after my first wet dream. Held up the sticky bedsheets and all. That's the kind of thing you hide, though.

"It doesn't embarrass you if I talk about that, does it?" she asked.

"No, of course not. No," i said. Meaning "yes, intensely." But then i furrowed my brow like an anthropologist in the Amazon jungle taking serious field notes about something he's totally detached from, and i felt better.

She saw right through that disguise. "You guys. You want

the benefit of it," she said, "but you don't really want to get to know it."

Thank God she called it "it." If she had called it "her," i would have gotten up and walked out of the woods. Fast.

Please, could we talk about something else? i thought. And please don't lump me with all the other guys. Remember your haiku? Could i collect what you owe me now? Could it be that you excuse me from this conversation? She must have seen that thought in my eyes, because she did. She moved on.

"Then," she said, "my mom also has a whole lot of Bad Days she makes us observe: like Hiroshima Day, you know, the day of the first atom bomb, and Kennedy's assassination, and the Pasture Fire Day."

"When's that?"

"April fifth, I think."

"What does she do?"

"She lights candles. The ones in jars with pictures on them. We don't do candles outside of jars. She turns out all the lights. She tells stories and explains the meaning of the day to me, as if I haven't already heard it a hundred times."

"My parents do the same thing," i said.

"Light candles?"

"No. Repeat themselves. Explain stuff i already know."

"Oh. Yeah."

We both smiled about that. To think all parents did the same thing.

"Then she has personal Bad Days. She wakes up and I see her dragging around the kitchen or outside on the porch, like all her clothes were made of iron, and I say, 'Mom, are you having a Bad Day?' and she's like, 'Yes, can you tell?' "

"A Bad Day on Bonnyvale," i said. That's the name of her street. Actually i mentioned that earlier. There i go, repeating myself like my parents do.

She laughed. "I'll tell her that. She'll like that."

We moved close to each other, touching, while our feet were in the water. Out of the water, too, because like i said, you couldn't leave them in for too long. We kept doing that. Feet in the water, then out in the air.

Rose Anna kept talking. "She keeps going to all these doctors. She takes me with her sometimes."

i just looked at her and listened.

"Well, not <u>regular</u> doctors. Healers. You know, crystal people. Pendulum swingers. Aromatherapists. Cranial aura scrubbers."

It's funny. i could picture them all.

"They never give her what she wants. She'll go to one for a while, and then she hears about another one and starts going there. As if any of them can help."

"You don't think they can?" i asked her.

"Of course not. Well, maybe a little. I tell her to stop wasting all that money. Just take it and buy us a trip to some tropical island. Someplace that's dog-friendly, so Dash can go."

"Can i come too?"

Rose Anna looked at me hard. "Seriously. She should save her money. I've been thinking about it, and I know what's bothering her. I mean, besides the Fire and all."

"There's more?"

"Of course."

"How do you know?"

"I spend every day with her. She's my teacher. She tells me

about it. And what she doesn't tell me I can just see. Some part of her depression isn't real depression, I mean it doesn't really come from inside her. It's outside."

"Outside?"

"She's not the one who's sick. It's this whole freaking country. It's so sick it's almost dead. She's grieving about it. But all her grief is stuck inside her. Sometimes I wish she would just start hollering. I'd help her--we'd run around in the woods shrieking. Ripping our shirts."

i pictured Rose Anna and her mom doing that, scaring the deer and the bird-watchers, kids on school hikes.

Rose Anna took her feet out of the water for the tenth time. She'd been settled back against her favorite rock, but now she leaned forward.

"It's not her fault," she said. "Nobody knows how to grieve in this country. They don't make any noise. Nobody taught them how. I don't want to be that way."

"Me neither," i said. i knew about that. The stiff upper lip. Don't let anyone see you cry.

i thought about Ishi. When his mother died and he was the only Yahi left, he went howling with the coyotes and golden bears up on the side of Mount Lassen. i'll bet the white people down on the ranches couldn't tell it was a human joining in the chorus. What about me, if i was there lying in my bed, listening to the sounds in the night, would i have known it was him? Would i have sat up and listened and understood?

"It's so ridiculous," she said. "It's just going to get plugged up. Whatever you have inside you, good or bad--if it's that strong, you have to let it out."

i waited for her to go on.

We both watched our feet in the water, for the few seconds they could stand it. Then we just turned and looked at each other.

There was so much to see.

Her eyes were deep, like pools i could dive into.

"You look scared," she said. "Are you?"

"No."

i wasn't scared, but i could see how somebody could be.

Amoss leads Oona out of the blackened square. Up ahead, we see Solemn Andrew waiting in the shadow of an old wild apple tree. He's breathing heavily, and suddenly Oona realizes how hard it must be for an old salamander like him to make such a hike. His energy is all show, for the benefit of his young friends. Something is driving him. He'd be so much happier resting in a cool, damp hollow under some rock.

Oona: "Thanks for waiting."

Solemn Andrew, with his voice slower and more gravelly: "No problem. I needed to rest. That was a rough piece of ground."

Oona: "Still, I don't want to make us late."

He holds her in his wise old eyes for a while.

Solemn Andrew: "Visions are powerful things. When someone's having one, the rest of us have to wait."

So, he knew she was having a vision. How? She didn't want to ask him.

Oona: "Well, it's over."

Solemn Andrew: "Not all of it. Only the part that you saw. What I mean is, Oona, since you asked—"

—which I didn't, Oona thinks—

"—is that a vision like you just had, a vision shown only to

you, has a whole other part. How you think about it afterward, what you do with it."

He turns away, comes out of the shade, and sets off up the Owl's Head trail. Oona and Amoss have to hurry to keep up with him.

When they're all together again, Solemn Andrew says, "Amoss and I walked right by it. Didn't we?"

Amoss: "Right by what?"

Solemn Andrew: "See what I mean?"

21

We went back up to the deck to eat our sand-
wiches and gulp springwater. Right where i held her crying,
that's where we sat and ate.

"Have you ever gone there?" i asked her.

She flashed me that look that says, Okay, I'm supposed to
know what you're talking about, right? "Where?"

"To the Thompson Pasture. To the burned-out place. Or up
to Owl's Head."

"No."

"i'm game," i said. "What are we waiting for?"

She didn't answer right away, so i said, "Dash knows the way.
Don't you, Dash?" He thumped his tail. Dogs get tired of sitting around waiting.

"i'm kidding," i said. "There's a topo map inside. We could
find the way."

We went in and looked at the old green map stuck to a log.
It was all there: Franklin's farm. The stream. Someone had
drawn an x for our cabin. It was near a dotted line called "Old
Slave Road," which led to a corner if you went north. There

were a few little black squares where my mom's commune was, or used to be. And a road winding by it to the Pasture. Some wavy contours that meant a hill, with OWL'S HEAD MOUNTAIN in all caps. Nothing was more than a mile away. Easy to find. i stuck out my hand and gave her my best let's-go look.

Now <u>she</u> looked scared. Or at least reluctant. She sat down on the sofa and let me know she wouldn't be budging soon.

"I don't think I'm ready."

"Okay."

"I think I want to tell it first. I don't want to actually see the real thing yet. I'm afraid it'll all be different from what's always been in my mind. Do you understand?"

"Yes. i think so."

"My mom would come in every night and turn out my reading light and talk to me. She'd lie down next to me and tell me about the sixties and seventies, about the movement, and communes, farming, and the Fire--mostly about what it was like to be alive back then."

"My mom does, too." Not the lying down next to me part, but the storytelling.

"It's not fair," she said.

"What isn't?"

"You know--we missed it. It must have been awesome. All that hope--right in the middle of the war. Big protest marches, and soldiers trying to stop them, and people sticking flowers down rifle barrels. And feminism, and the environmental movement just beginning, and Martin Luther King, Malcolm X, the Beatles, psychedelics--everything started happening all at once, why can't we do that again . . ."

i was drifting with her words, trying to picture it, and picture myself somehow magically back in those times.

Then i thought about the guy who gave me the ROYAL. Thirty-five years ago, when he came home wounded. What did he think about all the longhairs and stoners, radicals, liberated women, freaks from India? Did he even recognize the place? We studied that when we did the Vietnam War. The country almost split apart.

It did split apart.

i have to go talk to that guy again.

When he said there was a story stuck, when he said he was too old, he meant it. We needed a whole new movement right now. With Rose Anna leading, of course. Not me. i don't like to be noticed, remember?

But Rose Anna could be out front. She'd want to be.

Then there was a lull, and the old sofa sagged us closer together. i was waiting for, and excited about, and afraid of, what would happen when we stopped talking. Afraid of when we'd both keep our words in.

She must have seen me thinking that, i'm sure she did, because she sat up straight and changed the subject. "Ask me what I've been studying in home-school," she said.

"What have you been studying in home-school?"

"Buddhism."

"To go with your Wiccan? Don't they cancel each other out?"

She ignored that. She said, "Do you know what the ultimate source of suffering is?"

"Pain? Pain makes you suffer."

"No," she said. "--I mean, the cause of pain <u>and</u> suffering!"

"i don't know, sin maybe?"

That got her laughing. "Not to the Buddhists. That's what it is for Catholics."

"All right," i said, stumped. "Tell me."

"It's desire. They call it craving."

"Oh." i sat there next to her, pretending like i didn't have a clue what she was talking about. Desire? Never heard of that. What is it?

She went on. "They say desire is this endless loop. You can't get out of it even when you get what you desire."

"Why is that?"

"Because as soon as you get what you want, you're going to want it again, or want more. And since you can never really be satisfied, you suffer. Or if you use up what you desired, you suffer even more."

i wanted to say, Try me, it'll be worth it, but i didn't.

But she knew what i was thinking. She looked at me seriously. Her face said, Victor, can you <u>really</u> listen to what I'm trying to tell you? Please.

i breathed out, which i guess meant, It's okay, i can handle this desire thing. No problem. i'll just curl up near you on the couch here and let it loop around inside me. Finish the story. About desire, but a different kind. You tell it and i'll go write it down.

Her mom went to Woodstock. Another thing i wish i had done. Jimi Hendrix doing "The Star-Spangled Banner" all twisted on his electric guitar, distorting it like no one had ever played it before, making it sound like what the words really say, only it's totally obvious he means bombs bursting in a

Vietnamese village and women and children burning--you can hear the bombs, and the screaming. When was that? 1969?

And the March on Washington. Two hundred fifty thousand people, totally against the war. Linking arms around the Pentagon, the biggest meanest office building in the world. Facing off against the National Guard. Chanting!

They wanted to levitate the Pentagon, rip it off its plumbing and wiring, its secret subsubbasements, float it off into space. Weirdest UFO the universe would ever see. Aliens scurrying to get out of the way.

Her mom was in that circle, two miles around, holding hands, holding breath, and waiting for it to rise up in the air--

She's still holding her breath. She moved to a commune. There were ten thousand of them all over the country. All of them under the radar. She stayed there for four years. Then her own life went up in flames.

If only she could scream like those Vietnamese women, but she can't. She can't wail, can't holler. When she opens her mouth, nothing comes out.

But it's not just her. How could a whole country go mute?

Rose Anna was crying, but it wasn't like before, out on the deck, when it was out of control. When I was holding her. This time it was deep and quiet, like how she was that first day coming up here together, with the maple leaves, and her wanting to, having to, <u>do</u> something, with a force that made her eyes start to glisten.

That's the whole story she told me. Well, told herself, really. i was sitting next to her, so i happened to hear.

i hope i got it right.

Okay. Here I am again.

I'm back typing. Me, Rose Anna. I have a whole morning free, and I came up here to work on my story. And I'm going to hide these pages again when I get the chance, so someday in the future you are in for a surprise.

Happy almost June! Wow, so much has happened.

Remember I said I would probably type only once? I was wrong.

Yes I'm here by myself. Yes Dash is guarding the fort. Yes, I'm dot dot dot

There's something about this machine, I can't keep away from it. Help stop it's calling me to its evil den in the woods.

Little girl come in, I'm over here in the bed, no need to knock, come in, take off your red cap. And your shawl. And your little shoes. And and and and--

Grandma, what Big Typing Keys you have!

It's not really a ROYAL typewriter at all. It's some kind of diabolical mind machine that the Vietnam soldier guy made in his basement, the basement I've actually <u>been</u> in. We used to go trick-or-treating up Greenleaf Street, and he and his wife would be out front. They'd go "Hey everyone, come into the haunted house," with a big fake scary laugh, and when we'd go in, they'd stay outside, guarding our candy bags.

We'd all be winding back and forth in the spider-webs and tripping on our costumes through these cloth tunnels in his basement with some mad horror music playing on his tape deck, and now I think I remember--a locked door! That must have been his black magic workshop, where he made this thing disguised as an old typewriter. From scratch.

It attracts you to it, gets you, doesn't let you go,

till you do or say the things it wants. It's probably got a camera hidden in it somewhere.

Whoa, that's an interesting thought. Look at me! XXXXXXX

Sorry.

Here goes:

Victor writes what happens, what I say and he says, and what we do together, but even though he's very good at getting it all down while it's fresh, it's not the whole story. Specifically, what I think you get when you read his pages is that I'm under some kind of house arrest--my mom is the jailer, and she's so terminally depressed that if I leave her alone for a minute longer than I promised, I'll come back and find her dangling from the beam on our back porch, and if I had any sense at all I would be so pissed off at her, I would run off and do stuff I shouldn't do, like drugs or violence or stealing a car, or screwing really awful boys, or getting involved in some tripped-out fantasy because my only friend is my dog, poor me, nobody my age even knows who I am, they've never seen me, well, no, but I've seen them--I follow their tracks and maybe peep in their windows. I see the things they do when they think they're all alone.

All of which is totally not true. My mom is my teacher. She wanted to be. That's the work she wanted to do. I did do school for a while, but it wasn't for me, I hated it. My mom <u>was</u> depressed, is depressed, but like I'm telling Victor, it's not all organic to her, and I'm used to it. I almost like it now when she has a bad day. I know that sounds awful, but it's true. It means she can't do a lesson with me. She'd rather sit and think or listen to music, and I get to go out and play, I still call it play but, you know, I'm out here studying and reading and tracking and writing.

Homeschooling is not what it was back in <u>Little</u> <u>House</u> <u>on</u> <u>the</u> <u>Prairie</u> days. The sisters sweeping up the kitchen and clearing the table and sitting there with their chalk and slates. Little cold toes on the dirt floor.

I mean, my dad teaches tech ed, so I've been doing computers since I was about six. I go up to the college with him and hang out in the film lab or the library. There's only about three hundred students, and everyone knows whose daughter I am, especially the guys--most of them are really sweet, not macho. Sometimes I even go to the student center for a coffee, and we talk--

What else? I take two dance classes a week downtown, jazz and African. I like some of the girls, the ones who aren't so brittle and skinny, we go to the bakery sometimes after class. Share one of those hazelnut thingies with the chocolate dip on both ends. I actually like to hear about school from them. Most of the girls respect me and don't make me feel like a freak cause i don't go to the high school. They think it's cool.

I've always been athletic. When I was really young I played rec department softball. Outfield because I can run fast. Mom liked to sit in the stands and watch, also help out at the drink stand. I used to love to look at her, she looked so happy in the sunshine. She definitely doesn't get out enough.

I am not like her.

Should I underline that? <u>I</u> <u>am</u> <u>not</u> <u>like</u> <u>her.</u>

I learned how to track at the Environmental Center. They run it in an old farmhouse that used to be owned by this really old woman who I never met, who was an obvious witch, what they call a crone, more lines on her face than an ice-skating rink. None of her children approved of her at all, so when she died and they went to hear the will, they found out that she'd left her whole farm to the newts and porcupines. She'd set up a non-profit to bring groups of townie schoolchildren out to be brainwashed with her wicked witch agenda, like protect the environment, find wild edibles and medicine plants, test the stream water for six different things, or take a buddy on the meadow walk and look for signs of global warming--

In the summer, I get to go away. Dad's home all the time with Mom. I go to this progressive camp that doesn't have any organized activities. We all get together in the first couple of days and decide what we want to do. The counselors are supposed to be more like facilitators. So like, if we decide we all want to go help the local farmers get their hay in, they'll work that out. Or, this summer, if we just want to sit under the Big Green Tree for two weeks and talk about teenage sexuality and AIDS and gender and racial stereotypes in the good old USA, they'll help us do that, they'll just be there to make sure that everyone gets heard and nobody feels exploited or pressured.

Or if we say we want to swim naked as a group, yes, I do mean boys and girls together, so we can stop being so hung up about our bodies, see what penises and vaginas really look like, what all the fuss is about, they'll say, Oooh-kayyy, and we'll spend a while getting mentally ready and then go do it. That's what we did last summer. Not every day of course.

I like camp, but I was already planning not to go back this year. I'd like to go to some city and get a job clearing out a vacant lot and planting a huge community garden. Work with kids. Teach ecology.

Not for the whole summer, though. Because, you know. Now I really want to be here.

22

We got up from the sofa. Almost the end of our long day. Time to go take one last toe-dip in the stream.

i was still waiting for my feet to get used to the cold water, but it wasn't going to happen. "Hey," i began, but then i kind of wished i hadn't, "why don't you do some of your witchcraft stuff and make us a hot spring, coming out of that rock ledge over there? It would feel way better on our feet."

She rolled her eyes at me. "Like, just wave my wand?"

"Yeah."

She looked at me like she was seeing me for the first time. "You think witching is just mumbo jumbo, don't you?"

Uh-oh, i thought, i'm in trouble now.

"i didn't say that--" i started, but she was already up. She was into her clogs in a second and starting to bushwhack god knows where. i grabbed my sneakers. There i was again, trying to throw them on and follow her at the same time--but she stopped all of a sudden and wheeled around--i just about crashed into her.

"You think it's brooms and black cats and pointy hats and

presto! Make a hot spring or, whoosh, throw a handful of glitter, make some beauty queen break out in pimples all of a sudden--huh?"

"i <u>never</u> said i thought that."

She snorted and kept walking, but slower. "Yeah, but i can tell you don't respect it. Damn. They got to you first. They programmed you."

"Who's they?" i asked, but i had an idea.

"You know. The guys. The <u>male</u> storytellers. They're everywhere, and they never ever shut up. Is that all your 'magic typewriter' can do? The same old boring story?"

"What do you mean?"

"I mean it's hard for us goddess people to even get a hearing. Get <u>one</u> story told. It's all guy stuff."

"All right," i said, trying to get her to stop and face me again. "i'll give you that, but when you finally do get a chance, it's all this juju fantasy stuff, you know, toadstools, fairies, rainbows, a holiday to celebrate your period, i mean really--"

Her look made me stop. i was just pulling her leg, but the truth of it, my reluctance to accept what she believed, was coming out of me from somewhere. It surprised me. Maybe i <u>had</u> been programmed.

She stared at me like i was some kind of lower life-form. Like it hadn't been worth following my track after all.

"Okay," she said. "I want to make sure I'm hearing this right: you think the Garden of Eden, and a talking snake, and the apple tree of knowledge, and full-grown Eve popping out of Adam's ribs while he's sleeping--"

"--Wait a minute!"

"--Shut up. And a talking burning bush, and a flaming red

devil with big goat horns and a three-pronged spear, and a vir-
gin birth, and bare-naked angels with ten-foot wingspans but
no visible sexual organs, that's not juju? Using your word, not
mine?"

"Well, maybe," i answered, but i was losing energy fast. "i
don't know! Lots of people believe it."

"You're hopeless."

"Maybe <u>you're</u> hopeless if you don't believe! Did you ever
think of that?" i could feel my face getting all hot.

Mr. Halliday, my social studies teacher, he told me once that
you can go back and look at all the signposts along where you
grew up--they're all marked--here's where i stopped believing
this, here's where i stopped believing that. i never understood
what he meant till now.

But i wasn't there, not yet. i'm not saying i totally accepted
everything literally, it's just, i'd never thought about it. But she
had. Now it was me almost crying, because i saw her leaping
over some edge where i wasn't ready to go.

Please. Please don't go somewhere i can't go with you--i
thought, but didn't say.

"Look," she said. "I didn't say I don't believe all that stuff.
Maybe I do. But I believe mine, too. I want to believe all
those stories. They've been around so long, there has to be
something there. In both of them. The Goddess and the God
story. So I'm into them both."

"Really?"

"Yes, really. But the one you believe in, Father Knows Best,
never lets anyone else sit at the table. And it causes war, rape,
ethnic cleansing, genocide, and while everyone's fighting each
other, no one notices that the Greenland ice cap is melting

and the maple trees are going to die, and we're all going to drown. Or burn. Or starve."

i couldn't make that leap with her. i just couldn't make the same connections.

"Come on; I'll show you something else I believe in," Rose Anna said.

She pulled me to where the stream made a big bend to the left and headed faster downhill. Did she know the whole woods? Had i been coming up here for years and never really noticed anything? Even when i thought i did?

At the bend there was a <u>huge</u> tree. It had roots wider than my whole body, stretched into the stream for a nonstop drink.

"It's a white ash," she said.

She pushed against it. i looked way up--even the upper branches looked thick and strong.

"Touch it, it's real," she said. "But it's also part of a pagan myth. In Norse mythology the biggest ash tree in the forest was the one that held up the sky. They called it Iskadrill or something like that. 'The World Ash.' This is it."

"This one?"

"Why not?"

Rose Anna stood on one side of it and i stood on the other. We hugged the trunk and tried to reach each other's fingertips, but we couldn't. Even without touching her, it felt incredible. The tree was so big.

"See, figuring our arm spans, and adding the space between, that makes it almost fourteen feet around at shoulder height," she said. "Go look up Big Trees. I'll bet this one's even bigger than the white ash on the list. It holds up the sky."

"What's Big Trees?" i asked her.

"It's the state list. Vermont keeps a list of all its biggest trees."

"Wow, we should tell them about this one."

"No we shouldn't."

"Right," i said. "It can be Our Big Tree."

Who would want a bunch of Big Tree groupies and tourists tromping by the cabin while we were trying to write, or think, or you know--

But it was neat that the state had that list. i wondered if it had other lists. Big rocks. Big waterfalls. Big mongrel dogs. Big used tire dumps. Big abandoned factories. Big zits.

We were still leaning on opposite sides of the tree. i couldn't see her or touch her, but i felt her there.

"i just realized something," i said. "i recognize this tree."

"From where?" she asked.

"From your story." The big ash tree Oona Newt rushed by when the water first took her away--i remembered how i had pictured it. So the tree existed in my head before i saw it. It grew out of her story.

Just then Rose Anna came around from her side. We leaned against the tree together, our arms around each other. i'm not sure how we got that way, or how she felt about it, but she didn't pull away. i needed that big tree to hold me up. My knees were useless. i needed roots and a trunk. Almost every inch of me was pressed against her.

i heard a sound from her i had never heard before. A kind of sigh.

Then the sigh stopped, because we kissed. We just suddenly were; i don't know whether it was her or me who started. Oh man--

It hit me like a shock, like, what i'd been imagining was all of a sudden there.

It was amazing.

i reached up with both hands and tangled my fingers gently in her hair, making sure they got good and lost in it, like in a labyrinth.

Rose Anna kept drumming her fingers up and down my back, spider-walking, like the first time we met.

Finally she pulled away, but gently. Licked her lips. Eyes gleaming.

"I can't wait to read about this," she said.

23

Still the same day. The sun wasn't even low yet, but we started down from the cabin.

We both must have been in some kind of state. i know i was. Just above the steep part, we remembered that we hadn't read each other's writing, so we stopped. The old hollow log there is big enough for sitting on, or leaning against if the ground is dry. So we sat and leaned, with our feet extending over the cliff edge. It was where i stopped that time, when my back really hurt, and thought about tossing the ROYAL over.

So, if this is a movie, it's a <u>road</u> movie now. You know, sunshine and an open highway. Of course it's different, because it's three salamanders, not Thelma and Louise, or Kermit and Fozzie going to Hollywood in the Studebaker, but there's still that road feeling, with a nice straight path heading up the hill. And some cool traveling music. The climb is uneventful. Newts move slowly, and they climb even more slowly.

Oona, of course, is thinking of the words Solemn Andrew said to her. It bothers her that he <u>assumed</u> that she had been having a vision, <u>assumed</u> that she was some kind of extraordinary newt that heard some earthshaking Call to Greatness, <u>assumed</u> that he, the Wise Old Male, knew exactly what the young innocent female was supposed to do with her life.

Oona is thinking that no one can possibly know who she really is. She says nothing about this, but as she walks she keeps warning herself to be more on her guard.

But just then they cross an old stone culvert where a stream gurgles under the trail. She looks to the right and sees a waterfall like the one she had left so far behind. It even has a bare root whipping about in the spray.

She flashes back to her waterfall. She remembers how the water used to drown out all her ordinary thoughts, and how the dancing up and down had made her feel so alive. She liked feeling different, different from everyone who thought they knew how she was supposed to be.

Now she looks at her two friends. They've always showed her total acceptance, trust, treated her as an equal. She smiles at the thought of the warning she just gave herself. Let down your guard, she thinks, and right away she feels so much better. And, she thinks, why don't I stop focusing on <u>me</u> so much—there's this meeting we have to go to. It's important. So much bigger than me.

Somehow we've heard her think all these thoughts. Now we just watch the three of them climb higher. We hear the sound of wind, sometimes water, music. Finally we see, from a bird's-eye view, the three newts turning a last switchback and coming out at the ridgetop in a big flat clearing, just below the knob of granite that gives the mountain its name.

We weren't supposed to comment, but while we were sitting there leaning against the log, a question popped into my head.

"Hey, do you remember when you said that there were two times you saw a salamander in an unusual place, and that's where your ideas came from, and the waterfall was the first?"

"Yes."

"So, is this like the second time?"

She looked really pleased. "You guessed it. It was on a mountaintop, Camel's Hump, up north--I was sitting there resting from the climb, and looking off at the view, and something made me look down next to me. You won't believe what I saw."

"What?"

"There was a newt just like Oona, sitting right beside me."

"Wow."

"She was right next to that brass GPS plaque they have on the summit. The benchmark? She looked like she'd just arrived, too."

i pictured it all. Rose Anna on top of the biggest open granite peak in the state. This bright red-orange newt sitting next to her. Making eye contact with her.

"Newts live in the forest. She was about a thousand feet above that," she said. "I figured she must have a really good reason to be there."

24

May 29

Another Saturday. i finally went back up Greenleaf Street. i needed to talk to the yard sale man. i took Claire along. i thought i should put some effort into helping her turn out all right. Get her to be more like Rose Anna--woodsy and all.

i said we could take a walk in the woods up there, after we stopped and talked with someone. She wanted to lie around and read her preteen magazines, eat Day-Glo gummy worms, and talk to her friends on the phone. But Mom made her go and i kind of yanked her out the door. She said a few things to me that were right on the edge of mean but i just let them go by. i don't know where she learned to talk like that.

We headed up Greenleaf toward the bike trails, where i was heading the day this all started. i wanted to make her feel good about being with me, you know, special time with the older brother, so i told her about the Vietnam vet and the pile of old stuff on his lawn. i didn't tell her about the typewriter, though, or about Rose Anna.

"Maybe he still has some cool stuff lying around," i said. Although i wasn't sure, because it had been more than a month.

She made a grunt that said a lot of things. Like, Why did I end up with this brother who's so weird? And, I don't really want to come on this walk. All in a one-syllable grunt.

We headed to the top of the street without talking. Passed one sale but kept on going. The guy was right there in his yard, still surrounded by stuff. Only this time he was lugging big black plastic bags of garbage out to the curb. There was another pile of bigger stuff stacked next to his pickup truck. And there was a For Sale sign stuck in the middle of his lawn.

He remembered me. "Victor," he said, putting down the bag. He had a neat flattop haircut, like you don't see much anymore. Kind of speckled blond and white. "How's that old typewriter? I wondered about you. What you been doin'?"

i shook his hand. "Not much."

"Who's the young lady?"

"This is my sister, Claire."

"Hi, Claire. I'm Oscar." He aimed his hand in her direction but half-heartedly, because on the way, he saw her expression and knew she wasn't going to shake it. She didn't.

"Hi," she said. She started to pinwheel her eyeballs, which meant, "Uh-oh, these two people are going to have a conversation, and I'm stuck here till it's over."

We stood there not quite connecting. Then Oscar invited Claire to go take a look at the pile by the garage door. It was big, almost a yard sale's worth.

"Salvation Army stuff. Maybe there's something ya might like."

She started to roll her eyes again, but i stopped her with a look, and she smiled innocently and went over. i was kind of worried about what she would find. i mean, look what happened to me.

i turned back to him. "Oscar, huh?"

"Yeah," he said. "What a name."

"It's not bad," i lied.

i really liked him. Oscar.

"Hey, haven't seen you up here in a while. You traveling in a different direction these days?"

"Right," i said. "Thanks to you."

He smiled knowingly. "That old ROYAL, huh?"

"Kind of."

i was a little nervous. He could see that. i'll bet he could also see right through me and knew why. It was on account of that deal we had made--that i had to come up and tell him some of the story.

"Hey, help me toss this stuff in the back of the truck, okay?" he said. "Gonna do a dump run later." So i did. It felt better having something to do.

"So, how's the writing going? Did you ever get that story out?"

"i'm not sure."

"What do you mean?" he asked. He stopped and looked at me.

"i mean, when you said there was a story stuck there, i was sort of hoping for something exciting, but what's coming out is really only about what's been happening to me since then."

"Has a lot happened?"

"Oh man, are you kidding? So much!" i said.

"And is it exciting?"

"Yeah. To me."

"So?" He looked at me like i still wasn't getting the point, like i was Imaginatively Challenged. i guess i was. He blew out a lot of air and shook his head. i'd seen that look before--on Rose Anna's face. When she was wondering if i was worth all her effort.

He made himself comfortable, sitting on his tailgate. It creaked. i wasn't sure it would hold, but it did.

"Okay," he began again. "Tell me if I'm getting this wrong. You're writing a lot, right?"

"Right."

"Ya ever done that before?"

"Not really."

"So, it's something new."

"Yeah."

"You like doing it?"

"Yeah, i do."

"But it's mostly about yourself. Where you've been, what you're doing, what you're thinking?"

"Yeah. All of that. Lots more, too."

"Are you being honest?"

"Totally. i mean, i think so."

"And you said it's exciting."

"Yeah."

"Any surprises?"

"Lots." Girl's face at the window, blue feather, long kiss by the World Ash tree.

He paused a bit. "Does that machine work all right?"

"Yeah, works fine. You did a great job."

"Has it taught you to look at things different?" he asked.

i thought, How does he know about all that? But i didn't have to ask him, because he just nodded toward his house.

"I bounce around them four walls a lot, Victor. I write some letters, I keep in touch with people. Putting your thoughts on paper, it makes you stop and notice stuff. Kind of slows you down."

"It does that to me, too," i said.

"So, I'm kinda dense," he said. "I don't see what's wrong."

"Nothing. It's just--"

"Just what?"

"Nothing," i said. i wanted to tell him that i felt kind of like i had been tricked--in a good way, but still. i was expecting a different kind of story. But nothing i thought about saying sounded like it was going to come out right, so i just went back to stowing things in the truck. i stood on the tailgate and he swung stuff up to me.

"Anyway," Oscar said. "That deal we made?"

"What deal?" i asked, as if i didn't know.

"You know, the one where you have to show me the story? Once you got it outta there?"

"Oh, that deal."

"Well, don't worry. You don't have to."

"Thanks."

He must have seen how relieved i was. "It got personal, didn't it?"

"Yeah. Big time," i said. "It sort of snuck up on me."

"So. I guess there's other people in it," he said. "In the story."

"Yeah. Actually, there's a girl in it." i could feel myself blushing. He didn't look at all surprised.

"You'll have to meet her someday," i said.

He grinned at me. "I maybe already have, if that's the one come up here yesterday."

"What?" You could have knocked me over. In fact, he almost did. i stopped paying attention for a second, and part of a bed frame whacked me across both knees.

"I was dubbing around in the yard here. Late afternoon. She come up the street, had a dog with her, no leash. I thought they were on their way to the town forest, but dang if she didn't turn and walk right up to me and start talkin'."

i nodded. Sounded just like Rose Anna.

"Curly hair," he said. "Lots of it."

"That's her."

"She's a pistol."

"Tell me about it," i said.

"She said she come up to see was I the guy with the haunted house, when she used to trick or treat. She said she thought I was, but her friend Victor didn't describe me enough, so she had to come see for herself. And also to thank me."

"To thank you?"

"Yeah. For that typewriter. Said you and she both use it."

"We <u>both</u> use it?" What was she talking about?

"--up in some log cabin."

"Yeah, but--"

"Said you don't know how to work the capital I though."

"That's not true!"

He had this huge smile. All over his face. Like he knew exactly why i avoided it.

My mind started racing--picturing her typing alone. Come on, what else did he know?

It was like he was reading my mind. His smile got even bigger. "Hey, you want to know what else she told me?"

My face must have turned beet red. i tried to sound nonchalant. "Sure."

"Said if it hadn't been for me, she'da never met you. So she came up to thank me for that, too." He touched his baseball hat. "Cap stretched out about two sizes when she said that."

i let out a big breath, about half the air in Vermont. "i guess i better come up here <u>with</u> her next time. That way i can watch out for what else she tells you."

He laughed about that but then he turned serious. "Yeah well bring her up soon or I'll be gone. Leavin' town." He pointed to the For Sale sign. "It oughta say 'Sold.' Signed the papers last week."

Oh. i was sorry about that. Really sorry.

When we finished loading the truck, i looked toward Claire. She was scrabbling through a pile of jigsaw puzzle boxes. The thousands-of-pieces kind. She held one up for me to see. It was a picture of a big Tibetan sand painting. A mandala.

i don't do puzzles. They drive me crazy. i'll start doing one and then i'll think about it, try to make the pieces fit, even when i'm not there. Turn them around in my mind. Funny, i didn't know she liked them.

"You can take it," Oscar called over to her. She smiled and bobbed her head up and down really fast. Then she sat down on the ground and started looking at some old books. That made me feel good, at least maybe she had the old book gene.

Oscar turned back to me. "This last winter got to me. Too long. Hurts my old war wounds, too."

"i can imagine," i said, even though i couldn't.

"My daughter's out in Arizona, she wants me closer to her. I was ready to go anyway. All my shouldas were catchin' up to me."

"Your shouldas?"

"Shoulda done this, shoulda done that. They found out where I live and they're not gonna let me alone. Figure if I go hide out in the desert, maybe I'll be lucky and they won't find me there."

He looked away for a second, like he wanted to get back to his cleanup. But i really wanted him to stop for a while more, i wanted him to tell me more about the war. See, we were in a war again, the country was. So i asked him a few questions, and that got him talking again. He was actually a good story-teller. Even Claire came back over to listen.

It was mostly not war stories he told, though. It was post-war. He's on this goodwill mission to the Vietnamese, says they're the nicest, quietest, smartest, most decent, forgiving people he's ever met. He went back on a guided tour. No jungle boots or M-16s. Just a bunch of ex-soldiers sitting two by two on a tour bus, looking out at the farmland through the windows.

No, he says, none of it makes any sense, why we hated the Vietnamese, why we ever went to war in the first place, why 55,000 American soldiers had to die, 55,000! Why we went over there and wasted thousands of square miles with our bombs and chemicals. Killed about two million Vietnamese. And they're still dying from the poisons. He can't understand it--and he was there.

The people from his company--most of them say they

would have voted against that war if they could have. Would have tried to stop it. Would never have gone if they knew then what they know now.

"See, Victor," he said, "people back home started shaking their fists at each other. That's what Vietnam did. Now it's happening all over again. If we can't start agreeing, we're doomed."

"That's the problem, isn't it?" i said.

"You'd think people would learn," he said. "But they're afraid. Real powerful people want us to hate each other. And hate the people over there, wherever over there is. It's the oldest story in the world. And I bought it."

i nodded. i wanted him to know i understood what he was saying. Some of us younger people did. At least two i could think of.

"That's my biggest shoulda," he said, "shoulda understood it better. Shoulda read up on it. Shoulda spoke up."

i kept nodding. i couldn't think what else to do or say. You don't just reach out and hug someone you barely know. i don't anyway.

"It's not like we didn't hear the other side of the story," he said. "There were signs all around."

"Protest signs?" i asked. i was thinking posters on sticks. You see people in front of the post office every Saturday with their signs. "Bring the Soldiers Home" and "No Blood for Oil."

"No, not that kind of sign," he said. "I mean like shopkeepers in Saigon looking at me with hate in their eyes"--he looked down at Claire--"little girls hiding when they saw me coming. Buddhist monks setting fire to themselves--"

Then he saw Claire's eyes flash, and he left that last one in the air unexplained. i knew about it from Mr. Halliday's class, though. These monks would set fire to themselves as a statement against the war. Soaked their clothes in gasoline first. But at least they were careful not to hurt anyone else.

Oscar looked around like, Now look what we did, ruined a good conversation--

"Enjoy that puzzle, Claire," he said. "Good to meet ya."

"Thanks," she said. "I'm going to start it today." She held out her hand for him to shake. She can surprise me sometimes. He shook it like it was the best thing that had happened to him all day.

"You must be a fine young girl, if you're anything like your brother."

"Thanks," we both said, at the same time. And then Claire looked up at me like there was suddenly something new to appreciate. Which is exactly how i was looking down at her.

Claire and i went up to the woods past Oscar's house. Funny, that was where i was going the day i stopped at his sale. Now i was finally getting there.

i thought, What would Rose Anna notice if she was here? i showed Claire a little vernal pool with some deer tracks around it. We turned over a lot of rocks, looking for newts. Had to settle for ants. They get really upset when you blow off their roof.

The jack-in-the-pulpit were out. Claire put some rosy quartz pieces in her pocket. i think she had a good time. We circled down through the trees and came out on Western Avenue.

Claire talked my ear off all the way back home, with the puzzle under her arm. It was windy. She always talks with her hands a lot, and she was trying to hold her hair down in the wind, so i was glad that the box was taped shut, because the last thing i wanted was all the pieces blowing up the street before she even had a chance to put them together.

She wanted to know about Oscar.

i told her, Yeah, Oscar is special. He gave me the typewriter and i carried it up to the cabin. i don't know, just because. But can you keep it a secret? Please? Yeah, i'll take you up there and show it to you. i don't know, soon.

i still couldn't tell her everything. There was this voice in my head saying, Don't, don't tell her about Rose Anna yet. Someday soon, but not today. It's like i was waiting for something to happen, i didn't know what, but i just didn't want to talk about it--

No. It was more like i was afraid if i started talking about her, i would break some kind of unspoken rule, or spell, and i'd get up to the cabin next time and nobody would be there.

i knew Rose Anna's mind. If she could circle herself ten years back in time, how easy would it be to, just, take herself away now? Would she even leave a sign that she had ever been there, or would she disappear without a trace? i'd search the whole cabin for a feather, or a goodbye note--

i'd run crazy through the woods, back down to Bonnyvale, and find her house boarded up. Vines all over it. Broken-down porch. i'd stand and holler up at her window. In the rain. i know which window's hers. Someone would tap my shoulder: That's the old Hoozywhat's place, son, been shut up for twenty years.

i saw a movie like that once.

Claire ran into the house ahead of me. i woke up from my daydream when i heard her calling, "Mom, look at the puzzle i got! Off this free pile. It's a Tibetan Mandola."

i laughed at how she pronounced it, but i also thought, Watch out for gifts from Oscar, Claire.

25

June 2

A few days later Rose Anna and i were back at the cabin. Sitting out on the deck. i was glad she still existed. She was writing furiously, like, Be quiet don't stop don't interrupt me. But i was really impatient. i wanted to talk--

"Hey i went up to see--"

"Shhh."

"So were you ever going to tell me--"

"Shhhhhhhh!"

"But--"

She never looked up, she just kept writing.

Oona Newt, and Amoss, and Solemn Andrew are in the clearing under Owl's Head Rock. The others are already there, waiting for them. But we can't see them. We just see their signs.

The problem is, like Solemn Andrew said, no one has ever actually seen a sylph, an undine, or even a gnome. It's not like you can stand on the beach and a wave breaks and you go, Undine, are you in there hiding in the foam? Hold still for a minute—

Or go to Kansas, wait for a tornado, reach into the funnel as it roars by. Pull out a sylph? I don't think so.

They live in their elements. Not meant to be seen.

The meeting ground has been swept. You see a birch-twig broom leaning against the base of Owl's Head Rock, next to a pile of dry sweepings. And there are crisscrossed twig patterns left in the ground. So the gnomes must be around somewhere.

Then partway up the rock, in a deep crack, you see what looks like a pair of gleaming eyes. There's a powerful aroma of moss and soil that hangs about, like the sweet smell you get when you pull up a sassafras sapling and hold the root right under your nose, but how do you show that in a film?

Solemn Andrew calls out, "Hello?"

"Hello to you, too" comes a growl from the darkness, where the eyes are gleaming out.

Solemn Andrew: "It's good to, uh, see you again," he says, but he uses a fake voice, like what he really means is, We can't see you.

"You, too," says the voice.

"And the others?" Solemn Andrew asks.

"Oh, they're here." The voice from the shadow kind of chuckles.

It's nearly sunset. Sylph and Undine are not in sight, but they're both shape-shifters. They appear when you don't expect them. And in a form you may not expect.

Oona whispers, "If the humans need our help so bad, why is everything taking so long?"

But then she catches the concern in the air. We can do that with music and light change. Like a cloud. She smells something strange, too. She's lifting her nostrils to test the air. Not that you can actually smell carbon dioxide emissions, but that's the idea.

It's like the calm before the storm, like the main street in a western movie before all the cowboys jump out from behind the water troughs and start shooting—

Solemn Andrew calls out again, "Hello?" There's even an echo.

Oona can feel impatience coming from him now. They don't have much time. No one has told her specifically what the meeting is about, or how long it will last, but she has a feeling it will be short. No wasted words.

"I'm right here," says a voice.

It's the sylph. "Just don't look too hard," she says, "or I'll disappear." Her voice is quiet, like every whisper you've ever thought you heard in the wind.

This is not a threat, just an elemental fact. She's made herself into a rainbow—today—and they never last long. Especially not at the end of the day.

Suddenly Amoss interrupts with "Hurry! Over here!"

He is over near the big granite dome. Above him is the hollow where you can still see the gnome's eyes gleaming out. We move in close enough to see all the texture in the rock, and we see, nearby, a tiny trickle of water coming down. It's so small you can miss it the first couple of times you look. Then we follow it down the rock face into a little round pool, a natural bowl with stones around it.

Solemn Andrew: "That's Owl's Head Water. It's never gone dry."

Oona and Solemn Andrew head that way, too. The first real close-up of the pool could be from a neat, unexpected angle: like from inside the pool, looking up through the water's surface—all you see is water—with blue sky and clouds, and suddenly the three heads come into view from beyond the pool's edge. Their images are wavery, cause every drip that hits the pool makes the surface move, just a little.

Solemn Andrew is saying, "This place used to be famous long ago."

Oona: "Famous for what?"

Solemn Andrew: "Oh, you know, for spells. For curing sicknesses, for good harvests. The only other time I saw it, there were flowers and flags all around, and charms, and thank-you notes."

Oona says, "Right," but you can tell just from how she says that one word that she doesn't know. She thinks to herself, *There's so much I never knew. The boundaries of her old life were so small.*

Solemn Andrew's still talking. "It's not really a wishing well, it's not even a well, but this whole place, Owl's Head, the water, the ridgetop, had wishing power . . ."

As he's talking, we see this beautiful flashback—you could actually tell this whole scene from the water's point of view: have blossoms land in the pool, and young leaves, and seedpods, and a deer drinking, and autumn leaves, maybe a hand reaching in to clean out fallen leaves, so it's all the seasons passing that you see just on the water's surface. Even see it freeze over and thaw again. See the ice start thin, and go thick and opaque, and then in reverse.

In the non-frozen time, you can hear music playing like from a folk-dance group, and you see reflections of the dancers on the water. The music gets louder and the figures move and the prayer flags flutter, but it's all shown that way, in reflection. It's a vision of a day when people were happy because there was more magic, more folk music and dance, and more positive protest energy. It's *different from just wishing or leaving offerings at a magic well, it's actual fighting for a cause, with dance and music and love, everyone's involved, and then—*

Then the vision disappears, and we see the pool again for a few seconds the way it is now. Almost forgotten.

26

Sometimes i wonder what's holding Rose Anna back. Why isn't she roaming the woods right now, taking out the maple blight or whatever's killing the hemlocks, running north to hold the glaciers in their place and refreeze the pack ice so polar bears would still have somewhere to stand, not sink into slush up to their knees. Or zooming off to New Orleans or London or Bangladesh, any place at sea level, to get everyone to pile up sandbags. And gathering crowds and signs and flags and drums, and making her stump speech: Wake up! We absolutely have to wake up before it's too late!

i mean, i don't think i'm holding her back. She's just getting ready. It's the old caterpillar-in-the-cocoon thing.

"It's too hot out here," Rose Anna says, but she's not moving to get up and go back in the cabin.

"It feels good." i like the first really hot days of the year.

"Still," she says, "we can't ignore it, it's so obvious where we're heading."

We just sit with that thought awhile and don't take it further. She's at my side, hugging her knees. Head, curly hair, turned toward me sideways like that time up in the loft. Sparkling beads of sweat above her lips. i'm visualizing my arm reaching out and over her shoulder--she'll lean toward me--but i know i should just wait.

June is about waiting, isn't it? Time crawling. It's like the whole Northern Hemisphere reaches the top of the mountain of light it's been climbing, and everything, everyone, slows way down, waiting for something big to happen, for summer to hit, i guess, for school to let out, or, i don't know, waiting for the next disaster, next war--the next kiss . . .

Now every afternoon that we're together is just like that. We sit and feel time crawl, we lean our backs against the outsides of the logs. They're so warm, the sun's been baking them all day.

Rose Anna gets up and stretches in the heat. "You know what I would love to do?"

i don't ask.

She doesn't tell me, either. But i recognize her expression. It's the same one i saw back in April when she was peeking through the window.

Owl's Head Water is so tiny.

Part of it trickles down the rock face, through the moss, and part of it bubbles up inside the pool. The pool has a little natural rim around it, like a crater. Off to the right, there's a little nick on the rim where the water finally overflows and disappears again into the mountain. But not enough for a runoff stream. Just a dark wet stain on the ground.

The surface of the pool is never still enough to give a totally clear reflection. We get the feeling that we're looking right into Undine's soul, but she hasn't taken shape yet.

The three of them, Oona, Amoss, and Solemn Andrew, turn to call the sylph over to join them, but she's already right next to them. Rainbows move when you do.

When they turn back, they finally see Undine. We all do. Our water totem is a beautiful, wet woman now, in human form, sitting beside the pool like she's been there this whole time. She's wearing only a shiny skirt that looks to be made of dark feathers, like the cormorant skirt that the woman wears in Island of the Blue Dolphins.

Solemn Andrew says, "Hello, Undine."

She whispers a hello to them all. She has the saddest face. Lovely, but full of sorrow. She looks exhausted, her chest rising and falling, from hard work, from weariness.

She moves a little and leans all of her weight back against the granite. She gives a big sigh. The trickle of water pauses as it finds its path blocked by the top of her head, but after building up a little, it flows again, through her hair and down the middle of her head and forehead. It parts at her nose and runs down both cheeks, over her lips—we see her lips open slightly to swallow some of the water, and the rest goes down her chin, meeting strands of her hair again, and then down the valley between her breasts, her belly, and then divides again along many different feather paths all leading into the pool, her pool, Owl's Head Water.

Strength comes back to her when she swallows—she smiles slightly, nods slightly, as if she and the water are having a conversation no one else can hear. She lifts her legs and swings her bare feet into the water, and we hear her sigh as the coolness hits her.

Undine: "We'd better hurry. I don't have much time."

Oona: "Oh, are you all right?"

Undine: "I've had better days."

Oona: "Is there anything we can do?" She looks at Solemn Andrew, and he nods as if to say, Good question. Then Oona feels a whole rush of new feelings—new but somehow familiar—love for this beautiful being she has only just met; concern for everything she represents; and best of all, a thrill when she thinks about what she just said—anything <u>we</u> can do. She has never felt that kind of belonging before.

Undine looks down at her and tries to smile. She touches the top of Oona's head with her finger. As if she knows the exact place the waterfall always used to massage.

Undine: "I do need help. I've been working really hard."

The others, all of them, make quiet, sympathetic sounds around her.

Undine: "Oh, I'm not asking for sympathy." She smiles again with that same weak smile. A close-up on her face shows water moving down past her mouth. If we didn't know that it came from Owl's Head Water, we might think it was tears.

"It's just my bad luck," she says, "to be born on a water-cooled planet."

i do reach out finally. It's like i've just received a clear instruction. i rest my fingers above her forehead, and Rose Anna tilts her head up. With my thumb, i massage a place between her eyebrows. i make little circles, she closes her eyes, her whole face relaxes, then her shoulders. And her breathing.

"That feels so good," she says.

27

June 4

We're sitting back near the cliff top. On the hollow log, horseback style, but facing each other. Talking about a high school dance. What a thing to talk about with Rose Anna.

"It's called Spring Fling," i say. "Very original. Would you want to go?" My mother had heard people talking about it and thought we should go. Like it wasn't healthy for Rose Anna and me to be alone together so much.

"Maybe," she says. "Do you want to?"

It's funny, we can almost picture deciding to go, and getting ready, wearing something kind of outrageous, then meeting, being driven there.

We just can't visualize ourselves together, inside, with other people.

She hops off the log and starts up the trail. "It's the full moon that night, you know." We walk slow. June walking.

"It is?"

"Yeah. Check your almanac. The Strawberry Moon. The Full Rose Moon." She makes that last name sound so mysteri-

ous. And personal, too, like it's her own fullness. The Full
Rose Anna Moon.

i never even knew that full moons had names until a few
weeks ago. i mean, i used to go out and hardly notice the
moon. Used to.

Now, i'm noticing almost everything. And seeing signs, just
like she does.

*The camera moves back to Undine's eyes. And then to just one
of them. Super close-up. You see an incredible bright blue there,
like you see in a hollow under a glacier, in a sun-lighted crevasse,
and the blue is circling around the dark of her pupil. There are
sparkles circling, too, and picking up speed—like all the ocean
currents come together and accelerate at the top of the world,
where there's no land to stop them, and the icebergs circle around
in them, bright white against the blue. They ride around and
around, rising and sinking like the painted animals on a merry-
go-round. Big ancient chunks of polar ice that used to be packed
solid, now they're broken free—*

Polar ice.

Polar eyes.

Polarize.

Someone says that word out loud.

Probably Solemn Andrew.

*"That's what this meeting's about, isn't it?" Oona says. "Polar-
ization."*

*And her eyes widen. How do I know? she thinks to herself.
She looks at Amoss, but he doesn't seem to be getting all this. I
don't mean to imply that he's stupid or vacant or anything. He's
present, he sees what she sees, but it's like he misses some things.*

Maybe he's thinking on a different level, not a better or worse level, just different.

But he does ask a good question. "So when was the last one?"

"The last what?" *Solemn Andrew asks him back.*

"The last meeting."

"About fifty years ago." *The gnome's voice comes out of the dark. Oona had almost forgotten him.*

Solemn Andrew says, "It was right before that human woman wrote the book about the silent spring."

What's a silent spring? Oona wonders. Even the smallest spring makes a noise if you really listen.

"That was a powerful sign," *says Solemn Andrew. He's nodding slowly, remembering it.*

"What was?" *asks Oona.*

"Killing all those bald eagle babies," *the gnome says.* "If we hadn't done that, no one would have noticed."

Solemn Andrew sees Oona's bewilderment. He says, "Sometimes we have to do something to catch their attention."

"Whose?"

"The humans'. You see, for better or worse—"

"Worse!" *the gnome, the sylph, the undine say, loudly, all at once.*

Solemn Andrew gives one of his sad smiles. "For better or worse," *he repeats,* "the fate of the whole planet is in human hands. All we can do is call a meeting and put out a sign. A sign no one can ignore."

And while Solemn Andrew tells Oona about it in his wise old scientist voice, we see a montage of poison entering the water and the wind. Suddenly the light turns strange, and you can see stuff you can't normally see. And then up in the air you see big bald ea-

gles flying through it, and hunting, diving down into rivers and lakes and coming up with dripping fish, but somehow everything is discolored—you can see there's poison in the fish. And there's a pair of eagles, taking turns sitting on the eggs, then you see the eggs with the strange color, too.

And the chemical formulas for DDT and dioxin and fifty other environmental poisons would flash across the screen like the news does down at the bottom on TV when they think we need to see more than one thing at a time.

Then an egg starts to shake, and we watch a bald eagle chick with the colored chemical runoff in his brain trying to peck his way out of the shell, and you can see the huge legs and claws of his mother or dad right next to him on the nest, even trying to help, hear their voices, then he just dies half-born in a sticky heap of feathers and half-formed bones.

And there's music, and Solemn Andrew's voice-over: "Eagle wings that never soared. Talons that never gripped a cliff edge or a rabbit's neck. Eagle hunting cries that never carried on the wind."

We zoom closer to the deformed head, twisted to one side, half out of his shell, watch his eye just cloud over.

Solemn Andrew: "Silent spring, the woman called it. The one who wrote the book."

Undine nods, remembering. "That sign worked for a good long time."

"It was my idea," the gnome reminds them.

"Now we need a new one," the rainbow says.

28

June 11

Friday night comes. The Spring Fling. i tell my mother i'll ride over to Rose Anna's house on my bike. Her dad can drive us.

"Be home by eleven?" she says.

"It might be twelve, Mom."

"That's okay. We'll be up."

"i know."

They don't want me riding home that late, so i say, Yes, they can pick me and my bike up at Rose Anna's house, say at eleven-thirty. Maybe a little after, how's that?

My mom is on her hands and knees in our garden when i'm about to leave. In Vermont you have to garden like a whirlwind in May and June cause everything happens so fast. Aerobic planting and weeding. She looks up at me and i can tell she's thinking, You don't look like you're dressed for a dance. But she doesn't say it. She doesn't want to be caught not knowing about a fashion change she should have noticed.

We've eaten dinner. The full moon is already up, hanging all orange in the eastern sky.

"Don't get up," i say. And "Hey Dad, can i talk to you for a sec?"

It's a good strategy when dealing with parents to split them into two units and deal with them separately. There's a reason for this. It's like you enter into a conspiracy with one, in a friendly way, against the other. Meanwhile the other one has to sit there and wonder what to do or how to feel. It catches them off guard--should they feel left out, or should they feel proud that their child seems grownup enough to be asking for confidential advice?

"Dad, i'm not gonna lie to you," i say when we've walked a few steps away, down near a big old sugar maple. i put my hand on his shoulder, man to man. "i don't want to be caught in a lie."

"Thanks, Victor," he says. We're both standing on familiar ground: my legendary painful honesty. i think it comes with my name. That folksinger who always sang the total truth.

"We might not get to the dance tonight."

"No?" A really short word, but he makes it have tons of meaning.

"Dad, it's the full moon. Rose Anna really wants to be outside. She spends almost her whole life outside. i know we were going to go, but now we're not sure. i mean, we just might not want to go to the gym with all the people and the noise. All that loud music. We might just walk and talk."

He nods, taking it in. i want him to picture us sitting on a stone wall somewhere in town under a streetlight and talking for the whole time, maybe holding hands. Actually i make it seem more tentative than it is. So i guess i'm not being all that honest.

No, the more Rose Anna and i talked about it, no way were we going to that dance. On a night like this. We have a plan for something special.

Our staying away from the dance on the full moon night scares my dad. i can tell. It scares me, too.

My dad repeats, "Walk. And talk."

"Yes."

"Well, be careful, Vic." There's caution in his words but secret pride in his voice. He can't talk about it, but it's there. It's a guy thing. He's proud of me.

"i will."

He studies me. "You're not getting into anything over your head, are you?"

i think "over your head" is such a strange expression. Does it mean i'm about to drown? i picture myself gasping for air above some big water and my feet dangling, thrashing around helpless. But i don't feel that way. i feel just the opposite--floating, held up really strong, like nothing can sink me.

i see this new expression darken his face.

It's like he's suddenly thinking, If Victor's hanging out with just one girl, and they spend so much time alone together, they're gonna get involved. Really involved.

Or like he's thinking there's a talk he should have had with me, but now all of a sudden it's too late.

i shake my head. "No, Dad. Don't worry." But i don't think anything i say can really reassure him.

"Just be careful," he says, forgetting he already said that. There it is again, a girl is an undertow, and i'm about to lose my footing and get swept out to where i'll never get back. He's more scared now than i am, and i'm sorry for that.

Now there's one more thing to do. Claire's up on the porch working on her mandala puzzle. She's almost done. There are some holes in it but her groups of possible pieces are shrinking fast. i've helped her a little bit. It's almost every color you can think of, patterns interlaced and overlapped with other patterns, pulling you into the center and then whirling you back out to the edges again.

i don't think she's heard any of the conversation, but i think she should know, so i go up and hang with her for a minute, and i tell her most of what i've told them. Like, she's never heard of Rose Anna before. For Claire, Rose Anna wasn't there at all, and now all of a sudden she is.

"Why didn't you tell me about her?" she says. "You told me about all the other stuff." i'm afraid she'll start to cry, or dump the whole puzzle just to spite me. i don't know what would happen to us all if she did that. Those mandalas are powerful.

"You told <u>them</u>," she says, waving in the general direction of our mom and dad. Meaning, Whose side of the boundary are you on?

i lean right against her ear and whisper. "Hey. They don't know about the typewriter. Or Oscar."

"Oh." She makes that one word last for three syllables. Then, like she's satisfied, she smiles and gives me a goodbye wink. Now that she knows about Rose Anna, she's the only one with the whole story.

"Will you be home late?"

"Yeah."

"<u>Really</u> late?"

"Yeah."

The idea seems to thrill her. "See you in the morning."

So i'm forgiven. i say, "Let's do something tomorrow," and squeeze her shoulders.

"Ouch," she says. Then she leans over her puzzle again.

She doesn't chant--i don't think she knows how--but she's humming to herself. While she's pushing around a little cardboard piece with her fingertip. She has a private smile like she knows exactly what she's doing. She's not actually a Buddhist monk, she's a ten-year-old girl in soccer clothes. Her big brother is heading off into the unmapped wilderness by the Full Rose Anna Moon. But not to worry. She'll be back home keeping order in the universe.

i step off the porch.

My dad's still down by the maple.

We hug. i turn away and get on my bike. Start pedaling up the hill toward Western Ave. i don't look back, but i know exactly what'll happen. Mom will get up and brush off her knees and go ask him--So what did Victor say to you? She'll look for what's left of the conversation in Dad's eyes. Maybe they'll stand and watch me riding away. A metaphor. Then he can look at her and decide how much he'll tell her. i've left it up to him.

29

Riding over, i let all of that go. i'm free.

Rose Anna's story comes into my mind as i ride. It's starting to worry me. Like someone's going to die.

In the last part i read, a couple of days ago, night fell in the story, just like it's starting to now, and the gnome finally showed himself, he came out and built a big fire. With flint and sweepings and sticks. He had hairy knuckles and a big chest and was mossy like an old tree stump. Typical gnome. Right out of a Disney cartoon. Or one of those lawn statues. All the totem animals were illuminated by the firelight. But with Rose Anna and fire, i just have this feeling--

i lean my bike against her porch. i knock first, and then i go back and stand a little down her walkway to wait. Navajo Indians do that; i read it in a detective book once. Let the people inside know that you're there, and then let them come out when they're ready.

i have a view through the porch window to the front room. i see her mom rocking in a chair, her back turned. Why doesn't she come out? i wonder. What is she looking at? Is she reading?

None of my business, i guess.

After a while, Rose Anna and her father open the door. They stop to talk in the doorway. i can't hear what they're saying to each other. Dash comes out to greet me, and i pat his head. i'm acting real casual, like, Me and Rose Anna, we're just going for a walk. You can come, too. Dash, not her dad.

Her dad points to his watch, and she nods. He gives her a hug. Like the one my dad gave me. More than just a casual goodbye. Then she comes to the street and takes my hand.

Ooh, i think, that's for him. She wants him to see that.

We stand for a moment as if we're just now deciding whether to walk up the street or back down toward Franklin's place. We choose that way. Play acting for an audience of one.

"Great night for a walk!" i call back.

"We'll take Dash," Rose Anna tells him. Like she wants to reassure him. The family dog is a link to when she was little.

We walk right by Franklin's, go down to the corner on Western Ave. As soon as we're out of sight of her house, i stop for a moment to turn and look at her. A feeling takes me by surprise. Like suddenly my knees can't hold me up. They can't seem to do the job they were built to do. Walk, or even stand up.

Then they start working again--something to do with the way she squeezes my hand.

We window-shop for a minute in the few storefronts down by the blinking light. We don't go in. We don't want a photocopy, a slice of pizza, or a tattoo. We walk back up Bonnyvale and enter the field behind the milking shed where i first pushed my bike almost two months ago. i purposely don't look up the street toward Rose Anna's house, but if her dad is still watching from the porch and he sees us, i don't mind.

He is watching. i can feel it. Till the hedgerow blocks his view.

We cross the break in the stone wall and enter the trees. It's already getting dark in the woods. We're not worried about getting lost. We know the trail, and there's the full moon climbing higher.

The Full Strawberry Moon, the Full Rose Moon.

The full moon closest to the summer solstice. Maybe the most magical night of the year, in the woods. Rose Anna explains all this to me. The busiest time for spirits, like gnomes and fairies, which i don't really believe in, but that doesn't stop my enjoying stories about them.

We're almost running up the trail at first. Tonight is so close to the solstice it's almost the longest day of the year, which means the shortest night, which means if we have to be back by eleven-thirty, we'll have only a couple hours of pure darkness. Darkness is what we want, for our plan.

But then we slow down. There is absolutely nothing like walking in the forest in the moonlight. Why rush? And why make any noise? There are so many sounds to hear.

We can't possibly lose our way. There's the moonlight, and signposts on the road that i think no one else could read: the long hollow cherry log, the ledge over the drop, the part of the trail that's always wet. And there's fox fire--glowing places on rotten wood. They're like reflector strips on the side of a highway.

i don't think we say a word, the whole trip up. Dash stays real close to our feet. i keep bumping into him.

In the cabin, i light the lantern. You have to take it down from its nail, lift up the glass part, twist the wick up, and light it with a big wooden match. i do it really carefully.

i look around--i see the place is different. There's an Indian cloth on the table, and a bowl of fruit. Strawberries. There are wildflowers in a coffee can. A book with a feather bookmark. And candles in glass jars. We light all four of them.

"You were here today," i say. My voice croaks like on that first day. i must be nervous. But also, it's the first sound my mouth has made in fifteen minutes.

"Yes."

We both swing our backpacks off and lay our writing stuff down.

i'm amazed that she was here already, planning, preparing. My heart is beating really loud. i want to talk to cover the sound, thinking she must hear it. But she moves in for a kiss, quick and gentle, and then moves back, then reaches out and touches my mouth with her finger, one short dab, to be quiet, to quiet myself, to wait--

"Is this a test?" i ask. "Some kind of test?"

Rose Anna laughs. "No, not at all. We just have to wait."

"Wait?"

"Uh-huh."

"What for?" i ask. Till what? Or, because of what?

"I'm not sure. We'll see. We'll know."

"Some kind of sign?" i say. "Wait for a sign, like in your story?"

"Maybe," she says. "Yes."

"Okay."

"Okay then."

"Were you here writing?" i ask her.

"Yes," she says, like, Isn't that obvious?

*This next part is all shadows on the rock. Just like that other
scene was all reflections. Fire shadows: of the three newts, and
the gnome carrying bundles of wood, and Undine, one even of the
rainbow. Funny to think of a rainbow casting a shadow. But you
can do anything in a film.*

*The gnome shadow shuffles back and forth, carrying bigger
limbs, feeding the fire. Now there are big flames like there were
before in Oona's vision, and loud popping and crackling.*

*The fire makes Oona really nervous. But Amoss is right next
to her smiling like you do when you're sitting around a campfire.
He doesn't understand her complicated relationship with fire.*

*Then all of them talk about why they came there, how bad
everything is becoming with the planet heating up. It came on so
fast. They can't decide what to do. Would it be better to just let
the humans keep doing what they're doing? Let it play out? Logical consequences?*

*Oona feels like everything is taking so much time. She won-
ders why did she ever let these other newts sweep her along. And,
when is this meeting going to start? When are these old totem animals going to get in gear and do something if it's so important?*

*Then, as if she did speak, as if in response to her impatience,
Solemn Andrew looks at her. He gazes around at the mountaintop, trees, and sky, as if he was just going to say "beautiful
evening" or something like that.*

He moves quicker than Oona has ever seen him move: he leans all his weight back against his hind legs. His long tail bends like a birch sapling, and before Oona or anyone else can react, he jumps into the fire. And then he's gone. His whole life, and all his wisdom, disappear forever with a crackle and hiss into the center of the circle of fire. The last thing we see of him is the tip of his twitching, now-bright-red tail. Oona opens her mouth to scream but nothing comes out.

No one else moves. They're frozen: the gnome with an armful of branches he was just about to toss; Undine, exhausted, in the middle of an inbreath she can't finish; the sylph helplessly feeding the fire with her air; Amoss, up as high as his front legs can raise him, staring into the fire still smiling, waiting for his friend and teacher to make a magical return, to teach them all the lesson that goes with what he just did.

30

i put a piece of paper in the ROYAL and start typing, but nothing much comes. i'm still nervous, but i can't talk about it. A lot of time goes by. The few words i type, the machine sounds too loud. The keys are all stiff. You'd think that after all this time the ROYAL would loosen, but it's harder than ever to type. i wonder what old Oscar used to lubricate it.

But it's not the typewriter. It's my hands. They feel so heavy.

Meanwhile, Rose Anna's hunched over her paper, staring at it, as if she can see all her characters moving around there. i think she really can see them. Her eyes are all wide like she's watching a movie and she doesn't know what's going to happen next. Then i think, She <u>doesn't</u>. She doesn't know.

She writes for only a moment; there's this dry, scratchy noise, so she stops and fills the pen. Holds the little ink jar up in the light. Her grandmother's ink is almost gone. She looks at me. In the lantern light her eyes seem brighter than ever. She smiles, not in a teasing way, just, i don't know, calm, waiting.

Okay, send the sign, i think, so we can--

And right then, Dash barks. A loud warning bark like we've never heard him do before. Like he's been waiting all these weeks to do his job, so it's got to be big when it comes.

"Uh-oh," i say.

i get this feeling in the pit of my stomach. So sudden and scary. In the woods, in the night, your feelings can turn on a dime. There's nothing to scare you up here except other human beings. My mind runs to the wood-splitting axes in the tool closet. But i can't move. It's not just my hands that are heavy.

i think Rose Anna gets frightened too. Then, there's a sudden change in Dash's bark. It's quicker yelps now, and he runs to the top of the porch steps and sits there wagging his tail. i can see him through the window.

"It's my dad," she says.

"How do you know?"

"That's the bark Dash uses when my dad comes home. He must be whistling."

"Are you sure?"

"Yes."

"Did you know he was coming?"

"No. Not really," she says. Then, "Yes."

"Is he going to be angry?"

"About what?"

"That we're here. Like this."

She shakes her head. "I don't think so. He knew, sort of."

That surprises me. "What did he know?"

"Stuff." She doesn't explain any more.

"Well?"

"Well what?"

"What should we do?" i ask her.

She looks at me, like, Did you have to ask another obvious question, Mister Obvious Question Asker? "Sit here. Just like we always do. I write and you type. You get to the end of a line and make the bell ring. Then start a new one."

It seems like good advice.

The gnome keeps shaking his head and rocking his shoulders from side to side. We get a good long look at him for the first time. His mouth hangs down—brown teeth—and his jaw, which is all hairy, is shaking. Undine is breathing desperately; she's pushed herself away from the rock. She's on her knees now, cupping her hands, splashing what little water there is in the pool toward where her friend vanished. But there is too much fire and not enough water.

There's nothing the sylph can do either. Once a fire is under way, it sucks in all the air it's starving for, and more, till the solid fuel is gone.

Oona keeps blinking, as if she can squeeze what she just saw right out of her eyes—

i turn and look through the back window, and then i see his flashlight beam dance, just about the time i bet he sees the lantern light spill out of the cabin. He's not used to the woods like we are. He needs a light, even with the full moon. Grownups always bring along more stuff than they need.

i don't know what he's expecting to find.

"It must be beautiful," Rose Anna says.

"What?"

"Our lantern light. Fire in a jar. And candlelight. Spilling out of the cabin. Think how it must feel to come through the woods at night and see it. Like an old Russian fairy tale--"

"Yes," i say. And suddenly i can picture it in my mind.

"We didn't get to see it cause the cabin was dark when we got here. All we had was moonlight on the slate roof."

Moonlight on the slates. i hadn't even noticed that.

"Do you think something's wrong?" i ask her.

"I don't think so," she says. "No."

But i can tell she isn't totally sure. Maybe it's about her mom.

"Rose Anna?" his voice calls. Not a strong voice, kind of hesitating. i hear his foot stomp on the first step. i look out to the deck and see him bend down to say hi to Dash.

"In here, Daddy." Like a little kid hiding in a bed. Purposely calling him Daddy. See, dogs and bikes and names like Daddy are camouflage. You can hide behind them. From your parents. They'll look right at you but won't see you.

"Come on in. We're writing," she says.

i hear his steps along the deck, watch him walk by the window, and then he appears at the screen and comes in. He looks around at the whole downstairs. i smile innocently, like, Hey, i'm just sitting here working. Wow, look at that, i never even noticed your daughter's sitting here, too.

"We're both writing," she explains. We look up at him, interrupted at our work.

i pat the old ROYAL.

i'm ready to spin out a story about it if he asks. i'm a storyteller. But i figure she should take the lead here, and i wait.

She shows him her grandmother's pen. i think, Why don't you tell him in a few sentences what you're writing about? Say something. But she doesn't. Instead, she slides the page she's writing on nearer to where he can read it.

> *Solemn Andrew is not coming back. Ever.*
> *The old legend is a lie. There's nothing immortal about sala-*
> *manders in fire. They burn up like the rest of us. Oona is looking*
> *around for someplace to hide her head from the horrible popping,*
> *hissing, and crackling coming from the fire. But there's no way to*
> *get away from it.*
> *She hates fire, with all her heart. But she can't turn away, ei-*
> *ther; she's watching this wet smoky spout that twists up from the*
> *middle of the blaze. All that's left of the teacher. You can almost*
> *see a living thing in it. Or something that was living a moment*
> *ago.*
> *Undine is still on her hands and knees in the spring that be-*
> *longs to her. No more helpless handfuls of water. Nothing for her*
> *to do. Firelight glistening on her skin.*

Rose Anna's dad looks at her, nods his head without saying anything. He checks out the lantern. It started swinging a little on the beam when he walked in. Maybe he thinks it could fall down any second and send the log cabin up in flames. It wouldn't though, it's got a strong metal handle, made to hang even when a train thundered by, and the nail is thick and slanted upward. He reaches up and steadies it anyway.

He looks at the candles but they're all in glasses, and sitting on plates. For safety.

i think, How afraid of fire must you be?

You think fire gave her to you and is going to take her away someday? Then i realize no, he doesn't know about all that. Not in the same way i do.

i look up and watch the lantern light dancing high on the cabin ceiling. Through the cracks between the floorboards of the sleeping loft. We've never been back up there since that first day.

Suddenly he starts talking, nervously. Like everything he was thinking as he walked up alone in the woods has to come rushing out now.

He swears he wasn't suspicious, but he did see us head across the field, yes he was watching; no, of course he trusts her, me, us--he just couldn't stay put, the full moon and all, he wanted to take a walk, thought about it, wondered whether it would be snooping, decided it would be all right, he likes the forest, too, and it's kind of public land; well, actually, he wanted to talk to her about her mom, to thank Rose Anna, he says, and me, too, which i don't understand at all, and he's brought some cake and a thermos of tea, three camping cups, cause we're missing the refreshments at the dance, just for a walk in the woods; all right, he <u>was</u> nervous, well it wasn't just him who was nervous, it was Rose Anna's mom: more than nervous, with the full moon, you know, women and the moon, she was afraid, no exact reason, she just wanted to be sure that Rose Anna was okay. She sent him.

He brings us all this information in one long run-on sentence, and we just sit there and watch and listen and don't say anything.

i look at him and i feel like i can really see into him, not because i'm brilliant but because of the little bit Rose Anna's

told me. He's her father, of course, but it's more like he's her
guardian; he's supposed to take care of her for a while. But he
didn't make her. Somehow she came from somewhere else,
from her mother's stories, out of a fire like some mythical
beast--

Then i get this feeling, and i look closely at Rose Anna and i
can tell she's having it, too--that if we just ride out this conversation, which isn't even a conversation really since he's the
only one talking, that everything afterward is going to be all
right. This is what we had to wait for. To go through first.

Then, suddenly, it's all out of him.

"You want some chocolate cake?" he asks.

"Yeah, sure," we both say. "Great." More kid stuff to hide
behind. Cake.

We eat the cake and drink the mint tea. All three of us.

He takes a good look at my ROYAL. i tell him about how i
got it and how and why i brought it up here. He's a techie, so
he's interested.

He talks to me, and now we're two guys standing there doing shop talk, about my ROYAL's similarity to present-day
machines. He picks it up once. Says it's solid, like manufac-
tured things used to be, when American workers still went off
to a factory with their lunch boxes and made stuff that
weighed something. He points out all the recyclable metal
and glass, all made right here. When you're done with it, you
can reuse it all, grind it or melt it back down, make more steel,
make more glass, or toss it in a dump--not that you would--
and it good-old-fashioned rusts, would never clog a landfill
like a white plastic computer, he says.

He's not actually looking at me while he's talking. i'm listening to him, but it's all i can do not to shake my head. Human beings are strange, they hardly ever talk about what they really want to be--ought to be--talking about at any given moment. He didn't come crashing through the woods at night for this.

We didn't, either.

We're waiting for him to leave.

He came on the big spirit night, scared, looking for Rose Anna. Now he's got her right next to him, and she's not scared at all. There's nothing for him to do but pack up and walk back home.

He stops talking and looks at me. That drowning image hits me again. He didn't see this wave coming; now he's the one who can't keep his head up, he needs me to throw him something, a lifeline, a preserver, but i just don't think i'm supposed to.

She'll walk him out to the deck and hug him at the top of the steps.

i know, and i'm amazed that i know, and i don't know <u>how</u> i know, all these things. And when he reaches out to hug her, i know i'll be in the way.

Not physically in the way. i mean, i'm still in the cabin under the lantern. But somehow i get between them out there. On his side, there's some new feeling about her, that he never had before. And at that exact moment something on her side is-- what's a good word?--<u>braced</u> against his hug.

"Don't be late," i hear him say, loud enough so that i'll hear.

"No, I promise," she says. "Love you, Daddy." More camouflage.

i look through the back window where i first saw her face

and watch his flashlight bob up and down for a while and then disappear among the trees.

He's gone. i suddenly realize that it's finally night, as dark as it's going to get, because the moon is so bright. We don't have much time. Rose Anna comes back in and looks at me.

It's almost too much, that look, and i shut my eyes and just stand there waiting. Where will she touch me? My cheek, my hand? Then, when it's taking too long, i open my eyes.

There she is, back in her chair.

31

We're looking at the gnome again. He lets his armload of wood fall to the ground. He turns to Oona, to Amoss. His face is a mess of tears and dirt.

"I'm so sorry," he says. And then says it again to the rest of them, to no one in particular. His voice is high and broken up like bits of gravel tumbling down a hill.

The fire has almost died down. Oona feels Amoss standing close to her, touching her. He's beginning to understand that his teacher is gone.

Undine leans back heavily against Owl's Head again, breathing deep. "We need to finish this meeting," she says, with a great effort. "For Solemn Andrew. He would have wanted that."

Everyone agrees. No one really has the heart to go on, but they do.

We hear music come up now. Something violiny but almost religious, as if Solemn Andrew's death was a sacrifice that had to be made. Well, didn't <u>have</u> to be made—maybe he just chose to make it, like my mom's boyfriend. Why did he go into the fire? Did he think there was someone he could still save? Was he *working something out on his own? Either it went the way he planned or it didn't, but we'll never know cause he never came out to explain.*

And neither does Solemn Andrew. But his plan seems to work, cause it jump-starts the meeting, and his death is one more grief to add to the rest—Undine's grief that she can't keep up with the planet warming, that humans make her work so hard, they're so destructive, they never think about consequences. Add Sylph's sorrow for all the things she's forced to carry on the wind—she can't help it. Add the gnome's, the earth was such a gift to the human race, and now, who knows what's going to happen to it?

But grief can be an incredible source of energy. For good.

An idea comes into my head. i look across the table at Rose Anna. "So, is that why your mother didn't come outside?" i ask her.

"When?"

"Just now when we left your house?"

"What do you mean?"

"i mean, was she crying? Is that why she didn't come out?"

"Yes," she says. "She's been crying a lot lately."

i wait for her to explain.

"But it's not a bad thing. It's good."

That's all she says for a moment. She looks like she wants to ask me something important. Then she gets up and so do i and she pulls me over to sit on the sofa.

"Hey i'm still reading," i say, but she shushes me.

"Would you mind if I showed her my story?" she says. "I mean, my movie?"

"Of course not," i say right away. "Anyway, you don't have to ask; it's yours."

"Not all," she says. "There's a lot of you in it. But thank you. I'm really glad," she says.

"Why?"

"Because I did show it to her. I've been telling her about our writing together, and my wanting to get out, do something new, go to a regular school--"

"You do?" i say. "i didn't--"

"Let me finish. Lately she's had this look like she's coming out of a tunnel and blinking at the light. Maybe it's because of us, we're pulling her out. So today I thought, If her coming all the way out, and letting me go, is like a step-by-step thing, reading my story could be one of the steps."

"Nice."

"She got it all. She was like, You're right, we both need to get out of here. Then she just sat there with my story in her lap, like it was some treasure she had lost and just got back again--"

Rose Anna's sitting there looking at me, waiting till i get it, too. But i'm only thinking about her. i'm thinking how good she's going to feel with all that weight off of her.

Then it starts to dawn on me. "So, are things going to be different with us?"

She doesn't answer. She's waiting for me to follow the track by myself. Do my detective thing. She could save me some time and trouble but she won't.

Suddenly i feel afraid.

No more homeschooling. They're going to send Rose Anna far away. i just <u>know</u> it. Because she's so far ahead, or so differ-

ent, from all the other kids in town. That's what she's waiting
to tell me. i see it all in a flash--me taking a bus or train hun-
dreds of miles to go see her once a year. Her prep school. i'll
work some stupid job, bagging groceries, to pay for the trip.
Kissing her in a concrete stairwell. Or out in the snow. Staying
by myself in some stuffy guesthouse. Like a bad old movie. i
can already feel how miserable i'll be on the way home. My
mind starts running again, miles ahead--

But this time i slow down and tell her all the leaps my mind
takes, complete with the feelings, too.

She shakes her head. "Well, we talked about it. Mom and
Dad and me. That's what they thought at first, too." She
smiles. "But then I told them all about you."

That doesn't make sense.

"All about me?" i ask. i think, Oh no, if she told them--

"Well, not everything. There's stuff I would never talk
about, with anybody. Ever. You know that. But they said, Well,
if Windham High School turned Victor out, and he's anything like you say, it can't be too bad a place."

"Right," i say, although just now i can't think of anything i
do there except think about her.

i try to picture her in my school, but it's hard. i've only ever
seen her out in the fresh air, or in the log cabin. Could she be
happy in a painted concrete box? Moving only when the
buzzer tells her to? It's like she wouldn't be Rose Anna anymore.

But then, i try to see it from her side. All the new people
she'd meet, and have an impact on. i see the whole high
school, and everyone in it, changing cause she's there. The
town, too, and beyond--

i feel happy for her but sad for me. Or jealous. i know there's a shadow on my face. i can't hide it. i want to look away, but it's not a night for looking away. It's there for her to see.

We're not moving, hardly breathing. i keep meeting her eyes, hoping that she can't read all my bad thoughts, but then hoping she can, cause she'll know how to help me out of them.

i think she's trying to tell me, with her eyes only, that i don't have to worry, that we will still be best friends. More than best friends. But she doesn't say it. She just sits there kind of chewing on her lip.

What about our plan? i'm thinking. What we came up here for. Is this all we're going to do? And her look also says, I didn't forget. But this talk is another thing we have to get through first.

We both breathe out at the same time.

"So, yeah," Rose Anna says. "She was reading part of my story again, out loud to me and my dad. You did the right thing."

"What did i do?" i say.

She puts her arm around my shoulder and leans against me. "You waited. You knocked and then went back down the path."

32

Finally, then, the meeting really begins. The four totems review what's been happening around the world: coral reefs dying, freshwater snowpack disappearing on every continent, wildfires, drought, lightning in the Arctic, species going extinct faster than ever. And much more, all of it caused by humans.

And all over the world, the temperature rising. Steadily.

"What if we four worked together," the sylph's voice says. "If we took everything that's already happening and mixed it up into storms, all over the world?" She's getting excited. "We could have floods, and avalanches, and winds blowing where they never blew before."

"We do all that already," the gnome grumbles.

"But what if they were huge? What if we made them bigger than anyone has ever seen?"

"That might work," Undine says. "But we'd still have the problem."

Oona knows what that is. Solemn Andrew told them while they walked uphill. That most humans don't recognize a true sign when they see one. They used to be wiser. Now a truth can *stare them in the face, and they're too busy fighting each other to notice. That was the problem Undine meant.*

The sylph is right, Oona thinks. They would just have to show the humans power that they couldn't ignore.

Flash forward—to when the Big Storms come. People call them "perfect storms," almost with admiration.

And then you'd see <u>real</u> newsreel footage of hurricanes, and whole coastal cities wrecked like boats out on the ocean. Like the planet is taking revenge—

Because what's so different now is that every natural disaster is also man-made. Mudslides, broken levees, runaway sewage, tsunamis pummeling a shoreline that used to have a mangrove buffer. And clear-cut forests, houses on steep hillsides, big hotels perched on fragile beaches: the effect of every storm is so much worse because of what humans have done!

There'll be a scene of families clinging to a place they shouldn't be, eyes full of terror. And recordings of voices, like presidents or whatever, saying, "terrible natural disaster act of God dot dot dot," but we'll all know the real story.

They'll say, "Stay in your homes, duct-tape your picture windows, don't open the door, don't touch the phone, trust us, stay tuned, we're doin' a great job—"

Then there'll be close-ups of faces, and wind and water and fire and mud—all four—shattering windows, ripping things apart, and back to the faces as they get buried or burned or drowned, wiped out, screaming—

All the crazy sounds will crescendo, but there'll still be a few human voices of reason. From a few people who can read signs and know what they mean. Some of them even remember when the last sign was put out. They'll be hollering to anyone who will listen, trying to be heard above all the noise, "Look at what we humans have done! This is not just any storm! It's our own whirlwind."

Then the flash forward ends and we're back at the meeting, and Oona is saying, "We must do this, I know people will listen. They'll have to."

33

We don't have much time left.

The moon's moving up the sky toward the point where it'll be time to go home. It's already shining through the window on the roof.

We both know we want to--need to--look at the book on the table. Absolutely right now. Can't keep postponing it. We get up and open it to the blue feather, to the picture. Part of me can't believe that we're actually, finally, making this move.

We've each looked at the picture before, but never when we were together. We've avoided talking about it till this moment. i said we had a plan, but it wasn't spelled out.

"Do you think it's true?" she says, getting right to the point.

"What?" i ask, making her say it. Knowing she will.

"That you have to be naked."

"i don't know," i say. "i was just finding that out when you interrupted me."

"Sorry," she says, big fake dramatic apology.

"It's okay."

"Some interruption anyway." She smiles. "It sure took you a long time to notice I was back there."

She makes a long slow sound with her lips like when you're breathing over a spoon of hot soup. i take a swat at her and miss on purpose. Then we look at the picture again. It's pretty small, only part of a page, so we have to stand really close to look at it.

"One thing," i say. "He's all alone in the picture."

"So?"

"So he's complete," i say. "Also completely relaxed--you know what i mean. You put a girl, a naked girl especially, in the picture with him, off to the side there, but close, and--"

"And what?" she asks.

"--and it would be a different kind of picture, that's all."

She laughs. i love when she laughs. i've never heard anyone laugh so quick and loud without it making me feel like i was being made fun of.

"He wouldn't be able to concentrate," i say. "So how could he write?"

"You talking about him or you now?"

i have to be honest. "i guess me."

"Men," she says with a snort. "I thought you'd be different."

"What?"

"Like, always blaming us when they can't concentrate! Blame the nearest female."

i don't have an answer for that.

We look at each other. Who's going to make the first move? i remember what i thought and how afraid i felt when i first heard her come into the cabin, when i was hiding out up in the loft. Imagining what she was doing down there. Knowing she had read that book, had followed its instructions. Now, it's all different, and we've been waiting for this night, but still . . .

She senses my reluctance. No, "reluctance" is too kind. More like paralysis.

She lets out a big breath. Throws her hands up in the air. "I'll go outside," she says. Like, if this is just too much, I'll make it easier for you.

"Okay," i say. And out she goes.

As soon as she's gone, i take off my clothes. i pile them on the floor. Right away i start shivering. The chair is cold.

i didn't think it would be like this. i mean, when i pictured it in my imagination, we were together. i do all i can to meditate, to concentrate. i sit there and i try to write naked, but less than a page comes out, it's too distracting. i'm too out there. Definitely not under the radar.

i can't stop thinking about her outside on the deck with Dash. Both of them keeping guard. Looking out, not in. i think i liked it better when she was spying on me and i didn't know she was there. When she was just a tingle on the back of my neck. i hear her whispering to Dash, probably explaining what we're doing, and i think, If only i could hear what she's saying i would know how to be. We should have planned this better. This night is not working out like i thought.

i give up and put my pants back on. Just my pants. i have to.

"You can come in," i call out to her. Wondering if she will be disappointed.

"Are you decent?" she calls in, laughing. Then she comes back in. Looks at me. "My turn," she says.

i make a move to go outside but she stops me with, "No, it's okay, you can stay here." And she undresses. Completely.

Oh god.

It's the most beautiful thing--not a thing--i've ever seen. Full moon glow, lantern light, skin, curves, deep shadows, moving surfaces, alive. Nothing--no amount of imagining, fantasizing, looking at people out of the corner of my eye on the street, looking at magazine pictures, or paintings, or films, stuff on the Internet, no, or years of wondering how it will be, even dreaming--has prepared me for the shock, the beauty of it. That's it--total shock and total beauty at the same time. She stands still but rocks from side to side. Arms out. Hands turned up. Like she's saying, Well here I am. No hurry. Letting me see her. All of her. Even turns around and looks out the window as if something's out there she wants to see. But she is what there is to see.

i feel like i'm reaching for her like i've never reached for anything before. But i know i haven't moved. i'm standing still. i don't think i can move. i keep thinking we're not supposed to be doing this, i'm not supposed to be seeing this, and then i feel absolutely sure that i've crossed over some kind of line or barrier where "not supposed to" doesn't mean anything anymore--

She turns back toward me. i get this feeling like she's rushing at me like the ocean, pouring over a seawall in so many places and i'm the boy running up and down and trying to stop it, but there's no way, she's everywhere and i can't--

Neither of us is moving.

Then, finally, she does move--to her seat--and sits and leans over her paper and starts to write easily as if i wasn't even

there. She's completing her part of our experiment. She looks
totally relaxed. Like she's done this a dozen times before.
Oh.
i'm not going to think about that. Not now. Oh god.
Instead, i just think, How can she concentrate like that? But
that's the point, she's showing me that she can.

i sit down on my own chair, but i can't look away, i'm still
reaching out, and she is bending over the table, and sucking
the gold-plated cap of her fountain pen while she's writing
and thinking, miles away.

Well, not miles away really. See, the space in her story is
curved. Like she is.

> Then, the Summit Meeting is over. After they all decide what
> they have to do, they're so tired.
> You can see it in Oona's eyes: I wish I was home. She's never
> been away for this long before, and never slept on a mountaintop.
> It's not her habitat.
> But Undine looks so inviting. They find comfortable places on
> or against her, even the gnome, who's kind of shy. He leans near
> Undine. She rests her arm around him. They all fall asleep to the
> rising and falling rhythm of her breath like waves, or tide. Right
> at the bottom of the rock called Owl's Head. Right by the spring
> called Owl's Head Water. In the quiet, you can hear the water
> again. While what's left of the firelight fades into black.

34

She looks up once from her paper. Her eyes are wider than i've ever seen them. i want to stop time right here, but i can't. i want to get as close as humanly possible to her, but time is in the way, and the table's in the way, not to mention everything else--

i'm staring. i can't help it. She gives a big fake sigh.

She says, "You done looking yet?"

"No."

"Do you want to go out and look through the window?"

"No. This is fine."

"Try typing," she says.

"What could i possibly write about?"

"What you see."

So i do.

So does she. What i mean is, i'm convinced she really sees the things she's writing about--tracks and signs that no one else sees.

In the morning, Oona awakes to a scratching sound. Metal scraping on hard ground.

The gnome is over at the far side of the ridgetop. He's digging a narrow little trench all the way from that edge, back toward Owl's Head Water.

An aerial view would show this: Oona's very own stream is way down below that side, and then just past the big ash tree it takes a great curve, to travel around the mountain whose top she's on. It curves in an oxbow, a horseshoe shape, around to the beaver dam, the Pasture, and the black burned square. So she's not as far away from home as she thought. It's just a long way down.

The gnome keeps scratching with his hoe as the day gets lighter and lighter, and soon he's almost to where Undine is still lying, her body stretched out alongside the pool.

She hasn't moved a muscle yet cause she's actually holding back all the water that accumulated during the night, from the trickle down the rock and the little bubbling spring underneath. Undine says, "I can't hold back much longer, I have to release. Climb into the ditch, I'm going to give you two a ride down."

But Oona thinks, We're so high up. How can we possibly travel by water all that way down? Won't we get smashed, won't we drown? Who will guide us?

"Trust me," we hear Undine saying, with more energy than the day before. Oona and Amoss hang on the edge of the little ditch, uncertain.

Undine says, "I'll be with you all the way. You won't be able to see me, but I promise I'll be right there. Like I was yesterday."

"Yesterday?" asks Oona. "You were there?"

"Of course. Keep your heads up. Hold on. To each other, tight. I'll take you back to where you started, just below the—"

Her sentence never finishes. The last sound mixes with a huge

*outburst of bubbling water. It breaks past Undine's body; she to-
tally vanishes, no, shifts her shape, and Owl's Head Water races
into the trench, snatching the two newts as it speeds by.*

*The gnome—Oona glimpses him through a watery, rainbowy
curtain. He's smiling and waving goodbye with his hoe! His image is all ripply because her eyes are wet, and she's moving so fast,
and suddenly—wooosh—she and Amoss are over the side of the
mountain and tumbling down in a new little creek, scared, of
course, but holding on tight to each other. For Oona it's like a
flashback of her trip at the beginning, but now she's not holding a
dead piece of root, she's holding someone who's alive, and holding
her.*

*Together they ride over waterfalls—little ones—and bump
into rocks, and just make it through mazes of branches stuck in
the water, but Oona is totally confident that they're going to be
all right; she feels Undine holding them up and carrying them
down through all the steep zigzags.*

*So instead of trying to watch out and holler and steer and be
in charge, she just relaxes and lets herself go with the flow of the
water.*

Rose Anna finishes first. She puts the cap back on the pen,
picks up the paper, and makes a show of slamming it back
down on the table.

"I'm done," she announces. i nod, deliberately still looking
at the ROYAL. She slides her paper toward me. Then turns
slowly away to look out the window. i keep on typing. Maybe
just to prove something to myself. And to her.

When i pause she looks back around and says, "The guy was
right, you know."

"You think so?" i ask.

"It feels different anyway. Better. There's no place to hide. I think that's what he meant."

She seems to find that okay.

"Aren't you cold?" i ask her. It is the middle of the night after all.

"I don't think so," she says. "I can't really tell."

i think i understand her. i type a few sentences more.

"Let's read," i say then, pulling my page out of the machine.

"Are you done, too?" she asks.

"For tonight. Not with the whole story."

"Well, we know that," she says with a grin.

We read. Well, i mean i start. She looks at me intently while i read her first few sentences.

You know how you can be somewhere with one other person and feel like no one else in the whole world exists? Like everything, everyone else could dissolve and you two would still be there?

Oona lets herself feel that for just a moment.

And then she thinks about Solemn Andrew, and his wisdom, and the totem animals—everything she has seen, and everywhere she has gone. We'll see images of all that in the water she's riding in, showing up in the current, like quick highlights after the end of a film: faces and places you want to remember—

Oona is seeing this, too. She wishes she could hold on to every image and not have them rush by so fast. And then she wonders what she'll say in a few moments, when the other newts see her coming.

The tumbling water comes to rest all of a sudden in a peaceful eddy. There's a sound or a bubble or a wisp of mist that makes us know Undine is changing her shape and leaving. There's sunlight sparkling on the water. The tiniest wave propels them toward the shore.

Home. Tall hemlock trunks stretching upward out of sight. Green ferns curling over. Dew on every leaf. Deep brown forest floor. All these flashes of bright red and orange: the other newts are there watching, they were drawn to the place. Maybe one young curious newt, up and about before the others, noticed the new water source coming down the hill and spread the news—

Oona makes her way up the bank to where the others are waiting, with Amoss beside her.

How to begin?

"This is my friend," she'll tell them.

Because, in a great battle, you have to have a friend.

i don't know quite how it happens, but we finish with each other's stories at the same time. She's over there and i'm sitting here, leaning her manuscript against the keyboard of my ROYAL. She looks across the table at me and smiles. Then she stands up. And stretches. Slowly.

She starts walking over toward my side.

Oh my god--

Then she stops.

"Close your eyes," she says. "Cover your face."

"Like don't look?"

"Right."

i do what she says. i tell myself, Listen. Let sound tell everything. There's a night bird, and the water-- My hearing turns suddenly incredibly sharp, like a dog's, like a bat's. i hear her breathing, hear my heartbeat, hear Dash dreaming on the deck--

i hear her dressing.

It's the most exciting sound i've ever heard. i hear her bend over and pick her jeans up off the floor and pull them on, and

take a breath in to make them fit around her hips, i can picture that too, and then i actually hear the zipper move up
slowly and hit the top and then the button pass through the
buttonhole and flick once against her thumbnail, i guess, as
she snaps it into place. i can imagine what it all would look
like, but i don't open my eyes.

"Keep them closed," she whispers. "Arms down at your
sides."

i hear her step the rest of the way toward me. i keep my eyes
tight shut as she sits right on my lap, legs over mine, facing
me.

She puts her arms around me and squeezes so tight that my
breath explodes out of me. i keep my eyes closed. My face is
buried in the bottom of her neck. She smells so good. It takes
me a moment to realize why i didn't catch the sound of her
shirt going on.

i raise my hands and touch the cool, soft skin of her sides.

She is squeezing me so hard, pressing against me, pressing
my face against her, that i take it as a signal that she will not
be relaxing any time soon, will not let me pull back to look at
her or touch her. Not while she's this close. Not with my
hands. Not in front.

i thought breasts were supposed to be soft. i mean, that's
what i've read, or maybe i remember them that way from
when i was, you know, very young. But that's not what i feel
right now. Where she, hers, are pressing against me, i feel
pushed into, almost hollowed out.

Her cheek is against my forehead. We settle into each other,
chests against each other. She lets go for a moment, now she
threads her arms under mine and pulls me close to her again.

i'm held as tight as before, but now my arms are free to reach around and up. i take that as a kind of permission. i do the slow spider-walk on her back with both hands, all my fingers.

i let her know i'm deciding whether to go up or down. Down. Up. Down. i go up. Up is safer. She shivers. i move up the back of her neck, lose my fingers in her hair. Then to the top of her head. My fingertips get excited, feeling so close to, to what? to her mind?

Maybe she feels they're asking a question, my fingers. i mean, i'm sure i don't ask anything out loud, but she answers.

"I think I've got it figured out," she says.

"Mmmm," i say, kind of muffled against her skin. "i'm glad one of us has."

She presses on, more serious than me. "I mean, you've helped me. To figure it out."

"How's that?" i ask, leaning back just enough so i can look: look at her face, i mean, and also speak.

"With the ROYAL. You writing down the things I say. When I read it, I think, Did I really say that? I would have lost so much if you hadn't put it down."

"So, it's like i'm your secretary?" i ask.

"Right. My secretary." She grins, and i do too.

i could complain about that, or joke, but i don't mind. i change the subject. "So, i guess you're just keeping talking right now because you feel uncomfortable, being here like this? i mean, the way your dad was when he--"

"No. Let me finish," she says.

"Okay."

"Stop saying okay."

"Okay. I mean go on."

"And I'm not feeling uncomfortable."

"No."

"Definitely not."

"That's good," i say. "Neither am i. Well, a little bit." i'm thinking, i could use a little readjustment. i'm not going to explain that.

She ignores that and doesn't move.

"So what is it?" i ask.

"What is what?"

"What you figured out."

She doesn't answer right away. i go back to touching her hair and neck. i don't want to stop.

"Hold on," she says.

Like what Undine just told Oona and Amoss. How can two words mean so much? They can mean "grab on tight," for whatever reason; or they can mean "Wait a second, mister, stop, don't you go any further"; or "Stop time and remember this moment and get it all down in detail"; or "Don't give up, stay in the fight and keep your eye on the prize"; or "Hang on and strap in, cause we're taking off. Right now."

That last one: that must be what she meant.

We hold on. i close my eyes. Then i feel it. She must feel it, too. Something crazy starts happening to my body. i think the word "wow," and she laughs quickly in my ear as if she hears me.

We're taking off.

i feel myself rising right out of my body, looking down--i've read about this, like on a vision quest when you want your spirit to be set free. i used to think i knew what that would feel like--

But what i didn't realize is that it's not just out of body, it's off the planet, and i am absolutely soaring. It's so strange, tonight with Rose Anna i've just been feeling totally aware of my body, more <u>in</u> it than i've ever been in my whole life, and yet right now i'm totally out of it! i'm free of gravity, i'm <u>over</u> the radar, i'm not anywhere i used to think my "i" was. i'm more <u>naked</u> than i've ever been. Because nothing i was wrapped in is still there. My clothes. My old thoughts. My desire. My not-supposed-to's. Not even my skin and bones.

Suddenly i'm way up where you get a good view--not just of our two bodies in a log cabin sharing a chair, and not just of Vermont, or the earth, but of every planet in our neighborhood, the secret of space travel is solved and crossing any huge distance is possible, i understand it now, because time can suddenly shrink like a rubber band that was stretched long and tight for centuries and now suddenly snaps back small.

i can still hear Rose Anna breathing near me, but i can't even see her. Everything is rushing so fast i'm spinning, getting really dizzy. i should be terrified, but i'm too surprised to be scared--

Then, i open my eyes, and when i do i'm back, we're both back, still sitting how we were.

Whatever happened is over. But it's totally understood that we have both just been somewhere. Somewhere else. Instead of going as far as we could inside our bodies, which could have happened, almost did happen for all i know, somehow we went the other way.

"Did you--?" i say.

"Yeah."

"What just happened?" i ask her.

"I don't know."

Silence for a minute. i feel her relax a little.

"So," i ask, "that's what you figured out? Space travel?"

She just laughs. And nods, like she knows exactly what i mean.

i look up at the moon. We're almost out of time. Like we were just out of space. We can go a million light-years, but we can't stop the moon moving across its little part of the sky. i want us to sit here for hours more, but we can't. We have to keep our word. Now it's my turn to squeeze her hard. Like i'm trying to get that last little bit. i admit it. i do want more.

But i remember what Rose Anna said about desire. You have to learn to be near beauty without needing to have it. Without craving it, or using it up. Without insisting that it's there only for you, that it exists for you.

The lantern is burning way lower, and only one candle is left.

"I love this cabin," she says.

"i know." i always did, but so much more now.

i start my hand up and down her back again.

Then i think, Well, here goes.

i lean back to meet her eyes.

I tell her,

That's right.

I tell her:

"I really like your story."

"I like yours," she says. "Especially cause it's about us."

"You're what this place needs," I tell her.

"What place?"

"The earth. You know that. You see something little, but it's not little to you. A little trout pool in the woods means all the water all over the world."

"Well, it does." She pulls me back against her.

"Yeah, to you it does. That's how your mind works. You're the most watery person I know."

"I am?" She can't believe I just said that. And I can't believe she never noticed it before. All that fire stuff, that belonged to somebody else.

I go on. "Everything you see, you read so much into it. Your story is so full of imagination, and mine is about ordinary things, ordinary stuff, all right here."

Now it's her turn to pull back and look at me.

"Is this ordinary?" she asks. Eyebrows raised.

I shake my head no. Got me.

She stays leaning back, and now we actually do look at each other's bodies, freely. Arms lightly touching. Quiet again. Just breathing. She's glowing--it's the light from the last candle going out. Now there's just the lantern.

I don't want the night to end.

I take a slow look past her around the inside of the cabin. The book, propped open. The typewriter. What a machine. Not extinct, no way. Her gold pen. The nearly empty ink bottle. Two stacks of paper.

Everywhere, on all sides, the rough log walls. They get darker every year.

Then back to her. I don't want to, but I finish my looking. She leans in and rests her forehead on my head. We begin to rock, swaying actually, but very slightly. Together. A rhythm starting. Oh.

There's not a single part of me that isn't focused, isn't con-
centrated, toward her now. Touching her skin, tasting her kiss,
but trying not to rush, because I still want to notice, to put it
all somewhere inside me so strong that I'll never forget. But
still, each moment feels like it's building on the one before,
expanding. And she's right there with me--

Hold on, I think. Hold on. I want to stay just like this. I
don't want to go past. I don't want to use her or use her up.
How could I?

She must know exactly where my mind is.

"Is it okay," she asks gently, "if we don't go any further than
this?" Still rocking slowly. Pulling me close to her again.

I nod, against her.

"Is this enough?" she asks.

"Of course," I say. What does "enough" mean? I feel like we
have gone so far already.

I'm ready to do, or not do, exactly what she wants. How
could I do anything else?

"Are you disappointed?" she asks.

"No."

I'm relieved, but I don't have to say that. She knows.

Silence.

"They're like two parts of one thing, our stories," she suddenly says, in my ear, still squeezing me. "They complement
each other."

"What does that mean?"

"It means they fit together."

"Like this?" I ask her.

"Right," she says. I see her contented smile out of the corner of one eye. "They go together."

"Like us?" I ask.

"Like us."

Long silence. Finally I say, "We have to go."

"I know. I wish we didn't."

We stand up and both almost fall over; we have to lean on each other till our legs start to feel again.

Then we move almost in a dream--closing up the cabin, standing out on the deck.

Dash starts up, then slumps back down when he sees we're not quite ready. Our shirts and packs fall in a pile. There's one last thing--

We face each other. My legs press against hers. I touch her right above her hips, just where she curves back in.

Rose Anna's waist is cool and soft, I'm almost used to that now, but suddenly there's something else I feel, something incredible--it's like her skin is just the thinnest layer around a column of pure positive energy. It stuns me. In the next second I realize that nothing I'm touching, no part of it, no part of her, will ever belong to me in any way--in the exact instant I realize that, and my mind starts racing to find the right words to explain it to her, she reaches and links her two hands behind my neck.

Then--as if we've planned this, as if we've done this a thousand times--we each lean way back, in perfect balance. We look up together. No roof above our heads now. Moon and starlight pour down and fill the space between us, and keep pouring down over our hair, faces, skin.

It's like a waterfall.

*You never enjoy the world aright
till the sea itself flows in your veins,
and you are clothed with the heavens
and crowned with the stars.*
—thomas traherne (1660s)
the incredible string band (1960s)

ACKNOWLEDGMENTS

To:

Mollie Burke, for lifelong love and solidarity, and for her commitment to confronting climate change.

Maria Burke Gould and Willie Orlando Gould, for advice, companionship, and inspiration.

Eli Gould, for being, once, a teenage woodsman.

Margot and David Wizansky and Smokey Fuller, for building the log cabin in the woods.

My friends at the New England Youth Theatre, Governor's Institute of the Arts, and "Get Thee to the Funnery" Shakespeare camp, for uncounted hours of adolescent conversation, to which I really listen.

Alaina Hammond, for being a contrarian thinker, fine playwright, and my brilliant first reader. Howard Norman, for literary friendship and support. Deborah Luskin, Whitney Stern, and Andrew Marchev for insights and encouragement.

Melanie Kroupa, for extraordinary editing skills and patience.

Diane Gibbons, for being my tracking friend.

John, Ken, and Pat, for spiritual customer service at Black Mountain Print & Ship, Brattleboro.

The entire Vermont community of artists, performers, and writers, for making this state such a positive place to live and work.

Fellow communards at Packer Corners, for the decade we shared together on the farm.

Fans of <u>Burnt Toast</u>, for waiting so many years.

Thanks to you all.